Quest of the May's Rose

Kevin J. O'Brien

Matchstick Literary
1-888-306-8885
orders@matchliterary.com

Contents

Chapter One

On a dark cloudy winter night, a large boney white creature darting out and then back into the clouds flew over an Elvintown of Winter Strom (*Geimhreadh Stoirm* in Elvin) in the kingdom of Cynewyn.

The dragonlich felt a magic power from the town below him. He swooped into a diving attack and picked out the two largest buildings intown. He casted a fireball on both buildings.

As both fireballs hit their target, the dragonlich yelled out, "I'm Berubazius! Turn over my master's topaz or face your destruction!"

The whole town became alive with every bell ringing out and sounding horns calling of an alarm under attack. Townsfolks poured out of every building, many half-dressed and armed with the first weapon they could grab.

One of the townsfolks known as Dunbar Silverleaf shouted, "Men, rally around me! Get those women and children to the shelter!"As the women and children ran into a nearby stone building, Dunbar gathered his warriors from the third fighting regiment and townsfolks to man the town's defense to repeal the dragon lich.

Berubazius landed in the town's square breathing fire into the nearby group of warriors, killing many and wounding others.

Dunbar and the warriors he had gathered started to attack by arrows, spears, and magic spells like magic bolts and lighting.

Berubazius launched into an attack against Dunbar and a few warriors in the front line with his claws and bit, cutting down three warriors.

Dunbar and other warriors in the front line tried to surround Berubazius and attacked him, doing some damage to him.

Berubazius struckback with his tail. Hitting Dunbar in his chest, he threw him back about thirty feet.

Dunbar yelled out, "Warriors, attack! We need to kill or drive him out town," as he tried to get up, coughing up blood.

Berubazius spotted Dunbar and his sword. Rushing forward, the dragon lich hit Dunbar in his chest with his claw. Its pierced Dunbar. "So, you have my master's gem," Berubazius said, "Now I have it."

Several warriors and friends kept up the attack, pushing the dragon lich back from Dunbar by spells, arrows, and swords.

Berubazius fell back to the center of the town's square by all the hits from spells, arrows, and other weapons. Berubazius dropped to the ground and started to fall apart as his soul departed. He screamed, "I will be back!"

A young half-elf female ran to Dunbar. She was Dunbar's daughter. She started to bandage his wounds. His wounds were so bad that he knew he will not make it through the night.

Arimas, one of Dunbar's closest friends, touched her shoulder. "Elizabeth, I will help you take him home."

"Arimas," Elizabeth asked, "how bad is my father?"

"He is very bad," Arimas said. "Those wounds are very deep, and we have too many wounded."

"Is he dying?" Elizabeth asked.

"Yes," Arimas answered, turning to a group of warriors. "I need your help to take my friend to his home."

They came to Dunbar and helpedpick him up. They carried him to his home.

That morning, Elizabeth decided to write about her journey into her rite of passage to adulthood. The following is her story.

Chapter Two

My name is Elizabeth Rose Silverleaf. I am writing this tale on our planet Talamh, in the year 1310 of the second Common Era, on behalf of the brave and honorable men who made a long and dangerous journey to the Far East. We sailed west from the Port City of Fair Haven in the kingdom of West Thorne to open a new sea trade route to kingdoms of the Far East.

I was the miraculous product of an unlikely union in the village of Winter Storm in the Elvin kingdom of Cynewyn. My mother, May Fenwick, had a dalliance with one of the Elvin folks, Dunbar Silverleaf. As their only living offspring, I was raised by my mother and father until my eleventh year, when my mother died giving birth to my baby brother, Falcon. My brother died the same night.

My father decided that night to train me as a Warcaster. Because of the elfin blood that coursed within me, I became adept at the magical arts. He trained me for six years, until he was fatally wounded in a battle to defend Winter Storm against a dragon lich named Berubazius. On his deathbed, he gave me his Elvin chain mail, his masterwork long sword with a basket hilt, and the lands he owned. He told me, "Go to your uncle Isik Fenwick in the city of Fair Haven. He will protect you and guide you in the ways of his world."

The next day, I set out with everything I owned to the city of Fair Haven in the kingdom of West Thorne. I left the house and land in the hands of my father's close friend Arimas. On the day I arrived at my uncle's home, he had me attend as a witness to a meeting at the tavern Coral's Reef.On thatnight of Redleaves21 in the year of 1310, my uncle had gathered four other shipmasters and five merchants.

Captain Isik Fenwick, my mother's brother,was the master of *May's Rose*, his only ship, andowner of a three-story house, but he felt he had no legacy or lasting fame.Thirty years old, about six foot one, with light brown hair and dark blue eyes, he was one of the best-known shipmasters in Fair Haven. He hadno living family members but me, since the death of his wife from childbirth fever three years previous. His daughter soon followed her mother in death. He hoped to win great fame and wealth from this voyage and become one of the leading families in Fair Haven. *May's Rose*was athree-mastcarrackand known to be one of the fastest ships in Fair Haven.

As we entered the tavern, the cloyingly sweet scent of tobacco smoke from an elderly seaman's pipe wafted into my nose. Uncle Isik had always said that men of the sea were treated royally in this port. Now I knew it. Never had I seen a tavern so beautifully appointed. The candlelight illuminated gilded accents on the warm mahogany walls and shone brilliantly through a garden of flags. All of them, Uncle later told me, were trophies of war, courtesy of victorious captains. He led me past a group of merchant captains playing some sort of card game and through a heavy door into a large conference room.

By the light of the oil lamps he deftly lit, I saw the nautical paintings that covered the room, testament to scores of voyages to once unknown locales. He set one oil lamp on a green-clothed table with ten chairs ringing it. The second he placed on a smaller table. He pulled out one of the two seats and gestured to it.

"Sit ye here, good Bess," he said. "And utter ye not a word till I say otherwise."

As I lowered myself into the chair, I wondered about the empty seat facing me across the table. I wanted to ask Uncle who it was for, but I thought better of it.

As each of the men my uncle had invited entered the room, Uncle told me about them.

The first man who came in was Captain Eric Greenleaf of the three-mastcarrack*Spring Flower*.Hewasas tall as Isik and in his late thirties, with red and gray hair and light blue eyes.My uncle told me thatCaptain Greenleaf had made his fortune as a privateer in the last war against the kingdom of Gyrlac, and he bought the *Spring Flower* with that wealth he earned in the war. Captain Greenleaf stated that he hoped to come back with a new fortune, although he was a captain and businessman.

"A good sailor and navigator," my uncle added, "though he acts coldhearted. He's a good judge of men and knows what their capabilities are. Captain Greenleaf was one of Captain Dashwood's competitors in the wool trade."

"Greet you both," Captain Greenleaf said to us, "and well meet. Hope you two are well." He looked at my uncle. "Who is this lovely creature?"

My uncle said, "She is my sister's only living child, and she would never tell anyone about what is said in this meeting."

Byrne Warman arrived next, looked around, and walked straight over to Captain Greenleaf; he went straight to him and gave him a hug. Mr. Byrne Warman was of average height, about the same age as my uncle, with brown hair and brown eyes. As he asked Captain Greenleaf about this upcoming adventure, Isik explained to me that Warman had worked with Captain Greenleaf for the last eight years. In fact, he had backed Captain Greenleaf's privateering in the last war with the kingdom of Gyrlac.

After about five minutes, Captain Blain Evan Dashwood of the carrack *Mary Ann* came into the room. He too was tall and in his early thirties, with auburn hair and dark brown eyes. I was told that his family was one of the founding families of Fair Haven, and he was the second eldest in a family of nine children. He was the third-wealthiest person in Fair Haven, with a fleet of seven ships of various sizes and types. He hoped to prove that he was as good a sailor as his father was. I am judging by the weather marks on him from the sea and wind, as well as a smile with crow's feet on his face, it had been years if not decades he lived and worked on the sea. He showed his love for sailing and desire for adventure from the sparkles in his eyes and tone in his voice as he talked about the sea and places he had been. Few elves had such weather-beaten marks on their faces as Captain Dashwood.

"Captain Dashwood has been a shipmaster for seven years," my uncle said, "and is able to read the sea with as much ease as I can."

A few minutes later, Captain Armistead Hobert of the three-mast caravel *Gwenfred* and Mr. Ashdown Godsby came in. Both men were of medium height, with Captain Hobert appearing several years younger than the other men, with dark brown hair and brown eyes. As for Mr. Godsby, he was a half elfin his mid-thirties, with light brown hair and brown eyes.

Captain Dashwood, standing by my chair, told me that the two men had pooled their money to buy the *Gwenfred* from the family of her first shipmaster, who had died on her last voyage.

Captain Hobart greeted the other men and added, "My Alice has just told me that she is with our first child. And I know it will be a boy."

My uncle and Captain Dashwood shook his hand and patted him on the back for the great news.

Captain Jack Hawkins of the two-mastcog *Raven* arrived next. He was around six feet and in his mid-thirties, with black hair and brown eyes. Dress in a dark blue coat with bronze buttons and removable sleeves, as well as a big black hat with a peacock feather, he seemed to me to be a dandy. He had inherited the *Raven* four years earlier from his father. After he greeted the other men, he said he had found a backer for the voyage, a man named Mr. Blackwood.

Mr. Clovis Alsop Booth and Mr. Eager Warman, brother to Byrne Warman, came in together. I noted both men had blue eyes, though while Mr. Booth's hair was an ordinary brown, Eager Warman's was bright red. They were talking about the cost of the supplies they were going to need for the journey, and they kept talking about the cost to profit and the bottom line until the start of the meeting.

The last man to come in was the new backer, Mr. Bjorn Blackwood. He was older, an elf in his mid-fifties, with brown hair shot through with gray streaks in it. His eyes were blue, and he had a scar on the right side of his face. I had heard about him from my father. Mr. Blackwood was a famous elf ranger who was part of the last company that had made it to the Far East. The journey took three years and cost the lives of more than half of their company. My uncle stated that Mr. Blackwood represented one of the unknown financial backers for our journey to the Far East. He seemed to be cold and aloof to everyone.

With Mr. Blackwood's arrival, my uncle had me go to the bar and order four pitchers of beer and ale to be sent to the backroom.

When I returned to the room, everyone had taken a seat around the main table. They were still talking about anything except why they had come together. After the drinks and food had been delivered, my uncle ordered me to lock the door.

Captain Dashwood stood up and began to talk to my uncle in a cold tone. "We all were called to this secret meeting by you, Captain Fenwick. You have been talking about this foolish and dangerous adventure for months. You're asking us torisk our fortunes and lives on this journey by sailing west into the sea and into the unknown."

My uncle looked at everyone before speaking. "Aye, and a voyage to the wealth of the Far East by sailing on a new trade route. By being the first to see new lands and people, we will have the chance to establish new markets as well as finding new goods for our markets." He paused for a second. "That's why I called you all here, to ask for your help to fund this great adventure of our time. We all could become famous and rich, if you only have the will to grab it."

"To sail into the unknown," Captain Dashwood said to him. "Where we are going to find new friends or foes?"

"Aye. But we can make our fortunes from the new marketswe discover," Captain Fenwick said to the group.

"How long will this journey take?" Captain Greenleaf asked.

"I figure about a year or two at the longest," my uncle answered.

Captain Hobart set down his ale. "And what dangers do you believe we will run into?"

Eager Warman leaned forward to answer. "We figure there will be the normal dangers of the sea and the differences of the cultures in the lands we discover along the way."

"There are always dangers," Uncle Isik said, "and old and new dangers of the sea. We may encountersome dangers we have never seen beforeduring any sea voyage. Is this not true for all sailors who sailed the sea?" He waited for the other captains to nod. "But we are not strangers to the dangers of the sea and the unknown. We risk our lives every time we set to sea. It is our livelihood, is it not?"

"How much do yebelieve it will cost us to make this journey to the Far East?" Captain Hawkins asked.

Mr. Byrne Warman turned tohis brother. "Eager, how much do you think we can make from the adventure?"

"I figure the costs to be three hundred crowns for outfitting a ship with provisions and sailors, and an additional five hundred crowns for trade goods, for a total of about eight hundred crowns. But we could make ten toonehundred times the amount we spend." He turned to Mr. Blackwood. "How much profit did your company make on the last journey to the Far East, Mr. Blackwood?"

For what felt like minutes, there was no sound from anyone in the room. Instead of answering Eager Warman's question, Mr. Blackwood shouted,

"Does this include the cost of lives that would be lost? You all know the land route is too dangerous due to the bandits as well as the orc and goblin kingdoms that lie along the way to the Far East.I left many friends and comrades behind in graves when I made the previous journey to the Far East."In a calmer voice, he added, "But to answer your question, I made fifty thousand crowns in profit."

"Mr. Blackwood, what do the backers you represent think about this proposal?" Captain Hawkins asked.

"They believe this adventure must be undertaken, and theyare willing to provide athousand crowns and a Royal Trade Charter from the king.They do want tenpercent of the profit and any lands discovered that could be claimed for the Kingdom of West Thorne, as well as a map of all lands discovered.Is this acceptable to your company?"

"Who do you represent in this matter?"Mr. Godsby asked.

Mr. Blackwood answered, "They wish to remain unknown, but they are highly placed in the court of this kingdom."

Captain Dashwood looked surprised. "So,Captain Fenwick, you have been busy asking for support."

"Aye, I have been busy," my uncle said in a loud voice."And I am willing to risk my ship, fortune, and life.What about you?"

Anger chased the surprise from Captain Dashwood's face. "What about your niece?"

Captain Fenwick looked at me."I am willing to go," I said,"if you will let me, Uncle."

Captain Fenwick smiled at me and then turned back to the other men. "Well, I have a brave niece.She can control her fear.Is she braver than most of the men in this room?What about you? Are you just as brave as my niece?"

"All right," CaptainDashwood answered,though he still looked angry. "I will support and join you on this proposal.But you better be right. We will never live it down if we fail."

"You all are willing to form a company to make this journey?"my uncle asked.

"Aye!" they all called out, except for Mr. Blackwood.

"If we are so agreed," Captain Greenleaf said, "we need to pick a leader andadmiral general for this company."

His words broke the rest of the tension in the room. My uncle sat back in his chair and smiled.

Captain Hobart and Mr. Booth put forward Captain Dashwood's name.

Mr. Eager Warman suggestedCaptain Fenwick.

"Captain Hobart," Mr. Godsby asked, "don't you want to be in command of this company?"

Captain Hobart answered, "No, I want to be with my lovely wife before we leave.It may be years before I see her again, and I'd rather spend time with her than with you. The admiral general will have to spend a lot of time preparing for the journey and checking all ships to make sure they are seaworthy.I know he will get the lion's share of the glory and forever be famous, but he will deserve it."

"I vote for Captain Dashwood then," Mr. Godsby said.

"I vote for Captain Fenwick," Captain Greenleaf said.

"Captain Greenleaf," Byrne Warman said,"I usually trust your decisions, but I believe Captain Dashwood would be a better admiral general."

Captain Greenleaf nodded. "I accept yourreason."

"I do not know any of you," Mr. Blackwood said,"so I'll abstain in voting for who will lead you.But be certain you choose a good leader.You will need one with extraordinary abilities."

"I have the final vote to cast," Captain Hawkins said. "I choose Captain Dashwood as our leader of the company."

Captain Dashwood received the most votes, so he was made the leader of the company, with the title of admiral general. His ship, *Mary Ann*, would be the flagship of the fleet.

He nodded to Mr. Blackwood. "We accept your offer from your employer."

The men then all agreed on the goal for the company:to find a new sea trade route to the Far East.All believed they could make a fortune if they were successful.

After the other men had left, my uncle and I walked back to his house. "You are brave for your age," he said to me,"but still wet behind your ears.I know sailors, andmany are decent men, but a few are not.Likewise, with women. Some are crass and would take advantage of you.Because you have little knowledge of the world of man,I need you need to be under the eyes of someone who would not take advantage of you.Because of these reasons, I am forced to take you with me to truly protect you from the worst men, since I have no one I truly trust to leave you with."

"I been trained as a warrior and wizard by my father," I answered."I am not someone who runs at the first sign of trouble. I said I am willing to go! I have given you my word. I am the last of your kin. Please don't discredit me."

My uncle turned to me and laughed. "You are right. You have been trained to fight and live off the land. Now you will learn to live off the sea. If you go."

"Uncle, I—"

"My little Bess, we are home and it is late. Time to go to bed."

"Uncle, I ready and willing to go with you."

"I know, but you and I need to sleep now. We will talk in the morning," he answered me. "Now to bed, my sweet Bess. You are your mother's daughter, proud and brave to a fault, just like my big sister May."

Next morrow, I asked my uncle if he wanted eggs and bread for breakfast.

"Aye. I will have my eggs over easy. I've thought it over," he went on. "I will accept your word to go. I can't turn down—"

"Thank you!" I hugged him before he knew what had happened.

"You have to give up your female dress and wear a man's shirt and pant as a normal sailor," he said. "After breakfast, we will find you men's clothes and begin looking for good sailors. I know half of my crew will be willing to go, but the other half, I don't know about."

After finishing breakfast, we walked down to the waterfront. My uncle talked with his crew, and eighteen of them agreed to go on this journey to the Far East.

It was hard to find good sailors willing to go on such a long and dangerous voyage. It took weeks to crew up all the ships. In the end, the reputations of our captains and merchants won out. We were also able to sign on two other wizards and five healers. Our company finally numbered 120 for the journey, and all ships were fully equipped and supplied. I was the only female in the company, and I knew I needed to watch my actions lest I encourage any undue advances from the men. I would have a small cabin to myself, but this was a mixed blessing. I was protected from any unwelcome attentions from the rough sailors, yet I would feel like a prisoner cast upon the sea, with my uncle the jailor.

We all had a hard schedule every day before our voyage began. For four hours in the morning, we worked on readying all five ships. We had an hour break for lunch. After lunch, we had an hour of weapons training with swords and shields, two-handed weapons, and two weapon styles, and some of us had extra time with bows and arrows. Then back to repairing and replacing lines and sails until dark. Captain Dashwood believed there was a good chance we'd run into a battle with unknown foe, and he wanted us ready to handle any possible trouble. In the evenings, I had to learn nautical terms, how to read nautical maps, and how to tie knots.

The *May's Rose* was to be my new home. My uncle had sailed the sea since he was thirteen and had made ship's captain five years earlier. His first mate, Mr. Janvec Hill, had sailed with him for seventeen years; and he was a skilled sailor who could read the weather immediately, knowing it would change three hours before it happened. The second mate, Mr. Irvin Ashman, had a checkered past. He was a good sailor and was loyal to my uncle, who had saved his life. Third mate Mr. Dyce Pike was the brother of a shipmate from Captain Fenwick and Mr. Hill's first ship. Mr. Pike was known as a good sailor with a good sense of humor. He always had a joke or funny story to tell, some he called sea stories. The new pilot for the ship was Mr. Ervin Claymore, who was known as a skilled cartographer in the kingdom. He was also skilled in the arcane, or magic, arts. I was assigned as his apprentice, to be trained as a pilot and cartographer. The seventeen remaining crew was comprised of skilled sailors who had at least two years of experience under their belts. We also had a merchant and two guards on board, and room for three passengers.

Over the course of five months, we changed all the lines and sails on every ship in the company. It took hundreds of miles of ropes and unknown amount of canvas for new sails. Carpenters repaired the hulls and masts of the ships, each got a new coat of varnish and paint, and all the ships looked new. We also gathered supplies and cargo to trade or sell during the voyage. We included hundreds of iron bars; barrows of ale, whiskey, and wheat; jugs of wine; bundles of pelts, leather, and wool; glass works; and hardwood boards.

As the day of departure approached, all the ship's captains scrutinized every part of their ships, checking for any possible problems or uncompleted task. Even the slightest line off its belaying pin was noted and fitted. The day before departure, the entire company and their families and the financial backers feasted with a massive celebration, the likes of which I had seen only during my times visiting the Fair Folk with my father. The celebration was held in the town square, which had five trees in its center. Twenty tables were set up near the trees with an open fire pit, big enough for roasting a deer.

The day of the party was a clear and crisp in the month of Melting Snow. (My father always called it the End Winter.) Captain Greenleaf and Jane, his lovely wife of seventeen years, arrived just before my uncle and me. They brought their four daughters, who helped cook the deer and were on the lookout for husbands.

My uncle and I were next to arrive with two kegs of dark ale.Following us wasCaptainDashwood who arrived with numerous members of his family: his wife, Mary Ann, his wife of fourteen years;his younger brother Mr. Kyle Dashwood, who was his third mate, and their six children—the eldest, Aldwin, was his cabin boyjoined the party and helped serve beer from three kegs of local beer. His other five children were running around playing children's games.Captain Dashwood had proved to be a great dancer.

Mr. Ashdown Gadsby, Captain Hobart, and Alice Gadsby Hobart came with fresh-baked bread and pies. Mrs.Hobart's pregnancy wasstarting to show, and allthe company's women offered to watch over her while Captain Hobart was away.Captain Hobart had a sparkle in his eyes every time he looked at his wife.

Mr. Clovis Alsop Booth brought his wife, Charlotte, and their only two living children, along with baskets of cheese and fruits.His children'snames were Liam and Rebecca. He was a friend to Captain Blain and Mr. Kyle Dashwood. They sang songs through the whole party.He also had a powerful thirst for beer.He was always had a wooden beer mug.

Mr. Eager Warman brought his son Troy, his daughter Crystal, and his fiddle.Hewas a capable fiddler and singer and played all the favorite sea shanties. He seemed the sort of man who always had a smile on his face and a song in his heart, even though his wife had died three years earlier.

When Captain Jack Hawkins showed up, he wasdressed as a dandy again and brought along jugs of wine and kegs of beer.As he flung himself into the celebration, it was obvious he loved the young ladies, singing, and dancing. My uncle had told me Captain Hawkins believed he was under a bad luck cloud, and he hoped to change his luck and fortune with this voyage.Halfway through the celebration, he asked me to marry him, but my uncle had also warned me of what kind of man he was with the ladies, and I laughed him away. I watched him also propose to Rebecca Booth and Crystal Warman. Their fathers were not pleased about it.

Mr. Byrne Warman and Mr. Ashdown Gadsby brought more baskets ofbread and blocks of cheese.I had already heard the gossip that Mr. Byrne Warman chased any unmarried young woman in town.I thought Miss Joan was going to catch Mr. Byrne when he returned from the adventure.They looked like a perfect couple to me.

At noon the rest of the crew and their families arrived to enjoy a good time and to praise. The last to arrive was Mr. Bjorn Blackwood.He seemed aloof, even during just boisterous celebrants. To me, he seemed to feel like an outsider.

The whole crew ate their fill and sang and danced until dusk. Much praise was showered on the brave sailors, who were sailing off to face unknown dangers. It was obvious the families feared many of our company would never return. I danced with several sailors, both from the *May's Rose* and from the other ships. My best dancing partner was Mr. Gibbon Harwood, the second mate of the *Mary Ann*, who confided that he planned to marry again and become a ship's captain before he turned twenty-seven. As dusk arrived, the party ended, so the company could get some sleep before the start of our adventure. All gave good wishes and prayers for a safe voyage.

Everyone awoke early the next day and walked to the ships in silence, except for the crying of the wives and daughters. The crews boarded their ships, carrying last-minute needed belongings. Finally, we cast off. It was overcast, with a light rain moistening the decks, but the whole town turned out to see us off. I stood on the deck, peering back at friends and families just like the rest of the crew. The raindrops mingled with our tears, of both pride and sorrow. The wind was from the northeast, the tide was in, and the sea calm. Captain Dashwood gave the word, and all the crews jumped into action.

Captain Fenwick, our ship's master, looked back once and started calling out orders to his crew. Ready and waiting for his word, they manned their stations, hauling on lines, and set the sails with a purpose. Sea shanties came from every ship as we began the journey. As we rounded the jetty, all the crews took one last look at their families ashore. How many of them would able to see those wives, sons, daughters, and parents again? I glanced at my uncle, who was beaming, and threw him a warm smile. Under full sail, the *Mary Ann* led the flotilla out of port, followed by *Spring Flower*, *May's Rose*, *Gwenfred*, and the *Raven*.

After an hour, we cleared the lighthouse and were on the open, featureless sea. We had begun the adventure of a lifetime. We all knew it would be months, if not years, before our return. A part of me acknowledged, with a cold feeling in the pit of my stomach, that we might never return. For the rest of the day, we sailed southwest, making a good speed of about five knots.

Our pilot, Mr. Claymore, had told me to stitch a copy of his master map on a bolt of linen. While doing this, I learned how to read and make maps. He said he wanted me to have a copy of his map in case something happened to his master map. His master copy was also written on a bolt of linen that he used as the top sheet on his bunk. He informed me that if his master copy of the map were ever to be found by anyone from another kingdom, it would fetch a king's ransom.If a king of any land we sailed through found out hemade maps, they would keephim—and possibly me now—for the rest of our lives to keep the maps a secret from other kingdoms and to use them to expand their kingdom.We'd be trapped in one place, never to see new places and make new discoveries.

On the morrow, we encountered the town's fishing fleet returning home, their ships groaning with fish and the crews ready for rest.Our jaunty waves and salutes were returned in kind. These would be the last familiar souls we would see until we finally arrived home again.The rest of the day was partly cloudy, but what sun we did encountergraced us with its warmth upon our decks and faces. For a time, a pod of dolphins played comically near our ship's bow, and one of the men sighted sperm whales to the north of us.Over the next five days,we settled into a monotonousdaily routineof four hours on duty and four hours off, and everything seemed to be the same from one moment to another.To me, it felt as if I lived in waking dreamsfrom which I had no escape.

On the fifth day, Mr. Hill, the ship's first mate, stepped up to me and said, "I can tell yedon't have ye sea legs yet, me lass.Worry ye not. I've been sailing these seas for me entire life. I can tell ye true that every time I set foot on a ship; I fear it may be me last time. An' yet, she brings me home safe every voyage. And theMay's Rose is a lucky ship."

I couldn't begin to tell him how truly he spoke. Compared to the vastness of the blue ocean around us,I felt insignificant and small, a speck in the middle of a massive blue parchment.

My reverie and our conversation were cut short as the lookout sang out, "Ship to starboard!"

"Where away, Roland?"Mr. Hill yelled.

"Starboard fifteen degrees. She looks like she mayhap be a-taking on water, Mr. Hill," Roland shouted.

Mr. Hill ordered a sharp change in our direction to bring us closer to the ship.As we approached, I could see it in clearer detail. It looked to be a caravel, with her sails in tatters and one of her masts snapped in two, as if bitten through by an enormous monster.The clamor among the crew brought my uncleup from his cabin. With a practiced eye, he glanced over the wreck and seemed to know almost by instinct that there would be no living souls on board the shattered hulk.

"Away the ship's boat!" my uncle ordered."Mr. Hill, take six men and bring back any survivors ye find."

"Aye, Captain. We'll bringback all who are alive,"answered Mr. Hall. "Do ye think any are?"

"No, but ye know the unwritten law of the sea that all sailorsfollow, to give aid to a sailor in the water or crew of a sinking ship," said my uncle.

The whole company changed course toward the sinking caravel. It took an hour of tacking before we were finally alongside her to find her beached on a reef.Uncle and Mr. Hill both believed the ship had been there for over a month.

"Uncle," I asked,"why would you give any sailor aid,even if they were the enemy?What is this unwritten law of the sea?"

He smiled, and it was Mr. Pike who answered. "We all are sailors first, and they would give aid if we needed it. Besides,most of us can't swim."

"What?" I said."My father taught me to swim when I was five."

"Then you're one of the few that can swim.I can't even swim a stroke. Neither could my Pop, or my brothers."

Our longboat was manned, and Mr. Hill and five other sailors made up a boarding party.They boarded the wreck and found little of value.The ship's hull was cracked, and none of the crew could be found.Mr. Hill found the ship's log and the Captain's sea chest.He brought both back to the *May's Rose*. My uncle opened the chest and foundclothes and letters;a Trade Charter from the King of Gyrlac;a small sack of ten gems, each worth one hundredcrowns;a coffer full of ten gold coins and fifty silver coins from an unknown land (it turned out later they came from Tullian); and a working sextant.My uncleread the ship's log to see what had happened.After reading the log, he doubled the number of lookouts.

Chapter Three

The last entry in the *Zaria*'s log stated it was attacked by a giant squid, which had killed all the crew except for the first mate, John Cooper, and one other sailor named Peter. The giant squid had tried to crush and pull-down *Zaria* into a watery grave, along with her crew. With the ship damaged and taking on water, the first mate had crashed it on the reef to save the ship from sinking under their feet. He wrote in the log that the giant squid had followed them to the reef. Those were the last words he wrote.

"Uncle, how large do giant squids grow?" I asked.

"I seen one that was about five feet long," he answered, "but I've heard of one that was caught that was twenty longs."

For the next two days, everyone was on edge. One of the lookouts from the *Raven* spotted the beast and called out a warning just seconds before the squid attacked. Two of its long arms shot out of the water and rose along the *Raven*'s side. Towering out of the water, they started to engulf the ship. All but one of the crew was able to dodge the squid's strikes with its other tentacles. One of the cephalopod's suckers hit that sailor across his back and cut him to the bone. The crew grabbed any weapon at hand and started attacking the squid's arms. As Mr. Hill steered our Ship closer to aid the *Raven*, our crew was able to strike back with a volley of arrows. Ervin and I cast two magical energy bolts from our fingers. The *Raven*'s crew struck the squid with harpoons, arrows, axes, cutlasses, swords, and knives. They were trying to cut away the squid's arms, which had grabbed hold of the ship, but other arms were moving in to grab some of the crew. Two sailors were grabbed from behind and dragged over the side. We never saw them again. The *Raven's* wizard cast a spell that burned one of the squid's long arms, and another arm was severed by some of the other crew members. The tentacle fell to the deck, and four sailors threw it overboard. Still, the squid looked like it was crawling up the starboard side of the *Raven*, and that side was dipping into the sea. It grabbed another sailor and lifted it to its mouth, which snapped at the man, looking like a huge bird's beak. As sailors sliced and cut at the arm to free the sailor, Ervin and I cast more energy bolts.

"Man, your battle stations!" my uncle shouted, and every man on board grabbed his weapons. "Janvec, move us closer!"

"Aye, Captain!" Mr. Hill called back, "Steering *May's Rose* closer to the *Raven* so we could attack more directly."

Third Mate Pike and Seaman Wolfgang threw harpoons at the monster. Our training had paid off: both hit, but only one stuck.

The other ships were steering close as well. The *Mary Ann* had turned to port, swinging around to come to the aid of the *Raven*, but it took more than ten minutes before they were able to reach her. *Spring Flower* turned to the starboard, and *Gwenfred* turned leeward. All men who were not working the rigging and sails were firing arrows or throwing spears and harpoons at the squid.

Five harpoons and two dozen arrows struck the squid within a few minutes of the start of the attack. One arrow hit its left eye. The squid finally released the sailor and slipped back into the sea, releasing black ink to hide its retreat into the depths. The gods were watching over us that day. We were able to fight off the squid. Even more, the battle attracted another predator. A sixty-foot-long sperm whale attacked the squid from below as it tried to escape, killing it by crushing it between its jaws. The *Raven* appeared to still be seaworthy, but it had lost three men in the squid attack. All our nerves were on edge.

To help calm me and to give me something to do, Uncle suggested I try to decipher the *Zaria's* logbooks. I was amazed that the book had even survived the shipwreck. The red leather cover was badly damaged, and some of the pages had smears where the ink ran, but the supple vellum pages still yielded many secrets to me. The mention of my uncle's name early in the log caught my eye almost immediately:

> Month of Storms 15, 1311: 05:15. *Zaria*, under command of Captain Bryan Williams, set sail with *Griffon*, *Dolphin*, *Heidi*,and *Draigen* during light snow flurry cloudy day. Captain Rowen Loc of the *Griffon* in command of this expedition to Far East. We plan to be the first to the Far East and bet West Thorne expedition led by Captain Blair Dashwood and Captain Isik Fenwick. Captain Loc has informed me that Captain Greenleaf is part of the company, piss on him, and may he go straight to hell. He is a murdering pirate.
>
> 18:45. Weather turned bad; we have hit a winter storm. I have ordered safety line to be place around the deck.

So that was the game! *Zaria*had been part of a rival group, trying to beat us to the prize. Well, it was plain whom fate had truly destined for perdition, and I could not really shed a tear for their passing.

> Month of Ice1, 1311: 15:25. Our lookout spotted a strange ship South West near several pillars of rocks sticking out of the sea. The ship looked like merchant with single mast and two steering oars. She was under the command of Titus Claudius Romulus of Tullian.
>
> Month of Ice 28, 1311: 06:00. The morning sky was clear and fair winds and calm sea *with gentle waves from the South.*
>
> . . .
>
> *19:00*, I have taken command of *Zaria* as Captain, after Captain Williams was killed by Beast of death. Peter and I the last, the reast rest of the crew have been eaten by the beast. I have steard the *Zaria* onto the reef to save her from beening drag down to the watery grave. The beast had bit one mast in half and nearly drag the ship to the bottom. My port leg is gone, bit off just below my knee. Peter ask if any

find this log, please send word to his wife, Bertha, He love
her with his whole heart. He waits on the other side for her.
Sign John Cooper

After two weeks,allourships' captains and most of the first mates felt
the change in the weather.They ordered the crew to prepare the ships for a
storm by batting down hatches, placing lifelines, and checkingthat the cargo
was securely tied down. As we hit our first big storm, my uncle hadeveryone
whohadto be on deck or in the crow's nests tied onto thelifelines.We pumped
the bilges from the start of the storm until the end.The food during the
storm was hard bread and water.Most of the passengers and non-sailors were
seasick and bedridden.As for me, I manned the helm and worked on deck,
tying ropes and lines as they came loose.My uncle had forbidden me to go
up to the crow's nest, out of fearI would fall to my death on the deck or into
the sea.The sea scared the whole crewwith its enormous waves and its stormy
gray color. My uncle was at the helmmost of the time during the storm.Mr.
Claymore and I were unable to fix our location because we couldn't see the
stars.As for our personal conditions, we all were soaked to the bone and
exhaustedfrom pumping, resetting sails, or trying to steer.The waves were
twenty feet high or higher.The storm lasted five days. The other ships lost
seven men between them, bringing the total lossto eight men during the
storm.Despite my uncle'sactions to keep the crew safe, the *May's Rose* lost
one man, Root.A huge wave washed our deck and caught Root just as he was
crossing the deck.When the wave had past clear of the deck, Root was gone;
his safety line had snapped.

Duringthe week after the storm, we mourned our losses and repaired
the damages the best we could.I countedand mapped 107 tiny islands.About
seventy-five of them were just pillars of rocks, about twenty feet high and less
than fifty feet wide, with no signs oflife except for some seabirds and the grass
that clung to the sidesof the cliffs.Only thirty-two of themwereonly inches
above the sea.With luck, these islands would lead us to larger land ahead.

Chapter Four

S everal days after the storm had passed, we saw three fishing boats of a design we had never seen before.They must havebeen afraid of us, for they set sail as fast as they could.We followed them for three days before we sighted their homeland.It was a beautiful sight to seehillsides full of trees and white-walled multistory houses, and a twelve-foot-high wall for defense. We sailed to a small island just off the mouth of the harbor and anchored there.We sent one of *Mary Ann*'s longboatswith three of our merchants to see if the residentsmightbe willing to allow us to enter and conduct trade in their city. Our company hoped to establish docking and trading rights with anycity we came upon.One of our worries was that they might quarantine us.

As we waited for the merchants' return, I studied the defensive wall and noted that it had towers about every two hundred feet.Most of the homes beyond the wall looked like they were made out of blocks of stone or brick. Others looked as if they were made from plaster, with paintings decorating their walls.It took an hour for our longboat to return. They reported that theCityof Tullian had sent a letter to us, inviting us to dock at their port. Their letter started, "The People and Senate of Tullian send you greetings and welcome you to Tullian."They were willing to trade and sell us supplies so we could continue our journey. They stated that we were not allowed to sell any weapons of any type in the city. The captains also warned thewizards and healers to keep a low profile in the city. They worried the Tullians might fear our magic and unknown gods.

"Uncle, did you remember the *Zaria*?" I asked. "I think this is the city the logbook and letters were talking about."

"Ye maybe right.Keep your eyes open and try to find more information on Loc's company,"my uncle said before we raised the anchor to set sail into port.

Our fleet entered the port, and we sailed to our assigned dock. The dock was long and made of a strange stone that I had never seen before. We saw only a few of their ships in the harbor. They were of two types. One was smaller than the *May's Rose*, with a single mast and an open deck to store cargo, like the *Raven*. The other type was bigger and carried large pieces of heavy stones. Piled along the pier were strange jars that I learned were called amphorae.They were made frombaked clay, had handles at the mouth of the jar, and tapered down to their bottoms.The Tullians used these jars to carry different products, like we used wooden barrels.

As we disembarked, we were met by guards who followed us into the city. The city contained more people than I had ever seen in one place in my life. They wore a different style of clothes than I had seen as well. Men and women both wore what looked like a single piece of light cotton cloth. Their streets were made of stone, with walkways built higher than the streets.All shops were at street level, except for the ones in the market. The city's market had three floors of shops and was well stocked with fresh fruit and other goods, some of which I had never seen before.The city assigned troops to guard us from their people, and their people from us.

After we spent some time looking around and asking for translators, wewere introduced toa man who had two men, Arion and Hektor, who spoke our old common language and could act as translators. Their employer wanted thirty gold crowns for their services. They agreed to serve as our translators in Tullian as well as in Cleopatra. They didn't ask for any more money, just room and board. They seemed to be willing, if not eager, to sail on with us.

Mr. Claymore and I, with Hektor's help, located a local mapmaker who was willing to sell us some old maps. Those maps were expensive, but they expanded our knowledge of the new land. As it turned out, they were a big help later.

On our first night in port, we picked an inn near the pier where we were docked to use as a base of operationsas we explored the city. The inn was named for Poseidon's Daughter. It had good food and wine, as well as some loose women selling their wares to anyone who was willing to pay.

During the first night, two local men entered the inn. I noticed them because they were acting strangely, always looking around and keeping one of their hands inside their clothes, like they had a knife or another weapon. They called for drinks but never drank them. As one took a seat near the front door, the other walked around, asking our crew if they knew Mr. Ashman, who was our second mate. Eventually, he found Mr. Ashman, who was sitting with me. Through Arion, he said, "I was sent by Germoc Rowe, your old mate from the *Banshee*. He sent his regards, and he said you can help me. We need someone who knows about magic and can cast spells. If you don't have a spell caster, then any magical weapons or scrolls for sale."

"Why do ye want of me?" Mr. Ashman, through Arion, answered him. "Where is Germoc Rowe?" Mr. Ashman asked through Arion. "We may or may not have a spell caster in our company, but why should I help ye find one?"

I was near enough to them to hear most of the conversation and waited to see what might happen next. The man noticed me; I was dressed in my uncle's shirt and pants. Then he saw I was a woman by my chest, believed I was a woman, and he had nothing to worry about for I would want to deal the local authority. His culture believed a woman was the property of their father or husband, and he could be handled easily. By his custom, he had belief that women were trained to be subservient to men.

The man replied to Mr. Ashman, "I'm looking for someone who knows how to cast magic." The man said again, "Germoc Rowe said you would be coming with at least one sorcerer, and you owe him a favor. I am here to collect on that favor! Your spell casters are Ervin Claymore, pilot on *the May's Rose*, and Horton Noall on the *Raven*."

"Why should I help ye?" Mr. Ashman asked again. "What are ye really looking for?"

"I need one who can cast or make magic scrolls, potions, or magic items," he answered Irvin. "If your group doesn't have a spell caster willing to work for me, maybe you have some scrolls, potions, or magic weapons for sale."

Mr. Ashman laughed. "Sorry, I don't know if we have one who can make any magic items."

"What about spell casters in your company?" the man asked, his voice both deeper and louder.

Mr. Ashman answered, "We have some wizards in our company, but they're journeymen, and one master spell caster."

"One of them will do! You can make one of them willing to work for me!"

Mr. Ashman shook his head. "They are well paid and may not want to leave our company."

"I don't care," the man said. "You will make them work for me!I can match or beat their pay and provide women to satisfy their manly needs."

Both Mr. Ashman and I laughed at this.

"They may not want women as part of payment," Mr. Ashman said."One agreed to join us for some training by the master wizard, Mr. Claymore. The master wizard agreed for a particular bit of knowledge."

The man asked, "What particular knowledge was agreed to?"

Mr. Ashman answered, "I don't know, nor do I care. I was not there when the bargain was made."

The man asked, "How about the other journeyman spell caster, Horton Noall?"

Mr. Ashman stated, "I know little about thatone."

"What about the other one?" the man asked angrily. "The one I don't know about?"

"They are happy with the deal they made with the company," Irvin answered him. "Bess, don't ye agree?"

"Aye, Mr. Ashman," I said."You're right, the other wizard is happy with the deal, and I don't see anything this man can offer the other wizard."

The man glared at us. "I see you are part of the other wizard's deal and not willing to help me with him,"the man answeredangrily."Well, then,I'm still looking for magic weapons or scrolls with powerful combat spells."

"If we had such weapons," Mr. Ashman said,"why should we sell them to you?"

The man said, "I told you. You owe Germoc Rowe a favor and I'm here to collect it. Besides, I have a lot of money, and I can easily get more."

Mr. Ashman stated, "Too bad. We don't have any magic scrolls, potions, or weapons for sale. I have been looking for some myself.Maybe I can buy some from you, if you have any."

The man looked shocked. "What? Your people don't have any magic for sale? But didn't you come from a land full of magic?"

Mr. Ashman answered, "Our land has few master spell casters. Bess, don't you come from the kingdom of Cynewyn?"

I spoke up. "Aye, Cynewyn has many master wizards, a few Grand Master Wizards, and a lot of journeymenmagicusers—what you call spellcasters. I believe Cynewyn has more wizards than West Thorne. In fact, one of my father's half-brothers is Grand Master Wizard. He was able to cast several powerful spells,including Flaming Hell Stones. He established a school of magic in Winter Storm fifty years ago."

The man stared at me in disbelief. "You are pulling my leg. That would make him well over seventy years old. No man can live that long. And if he was your uncle, why didn't he give you any magic? Maybe you have magic weapons and items for sale?"

"My uncle is a middle age for an elf," I answered calmly. "Elves normally live on this earth for over two hundred and sixty years. He believed you must learn how to handle a spell before you can cast magic spells or make and useamagic item.He did teach me how to make a minor spell wand for single uses, like Blue Light or Sleep.But I don't have any of these wands at this time."

The man stood up and yelled something in his language at Mr. Ashman. Arion translated. "He said thank you for nothing. She is pretending to be a spell caster but can't be a spell caster! She is a woman.He says you two have played him as a fool! You wasted his time, and you can go straight to hell!He says he should kill both of you."

Mr. Ashman smiled and shook his head. "Then, go. Ye better not threaten us. Remember, we are armed and know how to use our weapons ina fight. Besides, we have spell casters that could kill you with a single spell."

As the man walked to the door, his facered withanger, he made a signal to the other man.

Mr. Ashman said angrily to Arion and me, "Germoc Roweis the one who owes me. And if he thinks I'm going against my Captain Fenwick or Mr. Hill, he is crazy. I owe them a debt that I have to them pay back! Now I must tell Captain Fenwick what just happened." As he stood up, he added, "This will ruin the rest of my night." Mr. Ashman smiled and winked at me in a playful wayand then walked over to where my uncle and Mr. Hill were sitting.

"Your uncle can't be that old," Arion said to me."You were pulling his leg?"

"Actually,my father's half-brother will betwo hundred and seventy-five next month, which is middle age for an elf. Elves can live for a thousand years or more, but that man does not need to know that," I said, almost laughing as I spoke.

I watched as the two local men walked to the inn's front door, apparently ready to leave. Before they could,one who was talking to Mr. Ashman and the other by the door tried to reach the door of the Inn to leave, but seven soldiers walked in and grabbed them. They led them away, and I never saw them again.As for Mr. Ashman, he came back laughing and carrying two mugs of wine, one for me and the other for himself.We had a good laugh at the two men's expense.For the rest of the time we were in Tullian, no one asked us for magic or weapons.

One of the good things about this city was that it hadseveralwhat they called bathhouses, and I could take a bath in peace during the time when women were allowed to use them. Of course, I had to change from my male attire to one of my dresses and act as a woman. Most of the local women stayed away from me,probably because I was of a different race and came from a faraway place they had never heard of. My father had told me that some people fear others who had strange looks, clothes, and habits.

The food was good but had a strange taste. I think it was the spices they used. I was able to purchase some spices for our use and for trade in later ports. I used some of them to help thefood on board taste better for the rest of the voyage. I later found out that one spice, a pungent sauce they called "*garum*," was made from fermented fish. The thought of how it was made, made me sick for two days after hearing that!

We stayed ten days for trade and ship repairs. While our merchants were making a profit from the sales of our trade goods, thecaptains knew they could make more profit by finding passengers to sail with us to the next port.

I asked around for information about Captain Loc's Company. I found that they had three ships similar to ours. They had sailed in from the East about two months ago.When they left, one had sailed to the East and the other two to the West. I knewthe *Zaria* was the one that sailed east.The merchants I spoke to said they had not seen the two ships return from the port of Cleopatra. They warned me that Captain Loc's crew looked like capable fighters andwas aligned with one of the leading families of Tullian. They should not be trifled with. I reported to my uncle all the information I found, and heshared it with the other ships'captains.

While we were in the city, the Tullians received bad news from the port of Cleopatra. Part of their army had been attacked and suffered heavy losses. They were asking for replacement troops and a general. Criers were sent out to tell all available legionnaires to report to the barracks before dusk.Most of the Tullian merchant fleet was in other ports, and the Tullians asked if we could take on their troops.They were willing to pay well, so each of our ships had twenty or more soldiers and their equipment assigned to them.

We were able to find six sailors to partially replace our eleven lost men. When we sailed, nine merchant ships joined us. I did not trust the new crew members or the soldiers, so I kept my weapons near me. They acted like I was an easy woman and desired to have sex with them because I dressed like a man and live on a ship with an all-male crew. They pinched my ass and talked about joining me in my bed.I tried to keep away from them by staying in the crow's nest, quart deck, or my cabin.

For the next three days, the wind was good, and the sea was perfect. I learned that the Tullian had been attacked from the south near the port of Cleopatra. They had lost a Legion's General and five hundred troops.The new general we were transporting had been in charge of the Legion two years earlier. He was familiar with the territory and respected by the troops.

One of his staff also informed us that a pirate's fleet prowled the waters between the ports of Tullian and Cleopatra. After learning of this, my uncle ordered extra lookouts. On the fourth day, the morning sky was red. Nine sails were spotted to the south, about a mile away and paralleling us. They stayed there for a few hours before they made their move. As they turned toward us, it started to rain. Too bad for them! Wehad expected their move and were prepared for them. When they showed their true colors, Ervin hit them with a spell of magical energythat burst into a ball of flames more than forty feet in diameter, and three of their galley ships were set on fire. They sank within the hour, with most of their sailors still onboard. The Tullian troops looked like they had seen a ghost. Most never had seen a spell before. Nor, I guessed, had the pirates. Some of our crew, including me, also hit them with arrows. Still they kept coming. The loss of the three ships and our defensive acts didn't seem to scare them or, indeed, to even matter to them. They kept coming. As they drew closer, Ervin hit them with a second spell. The magical fire of energy shaped in a ballstruck only two more of the pirate ships, leaving them burning and sinking.

After that, only one of the pirate ships pressed on and came alongside the *Raven*. No doubt the pirates were surprised to find Tullian legionnaires waiting to cut them down. The *Raven*'s wizard, Horton, cast two spells that caused some of the pirates to fall asleep as they boarded. Eleven of the pirates fell between the two ships. The remaining pirates swarmed the *Raven*, but the well-trained soldiers cut many of them down. After a bit of time, the *Raven*'s deck was awash with the blood of dead and dying pirates.

The remaining pirates on the *Raven* were forced to surrender. A few of the legionnaires were wounded, but none were killed during the engagement. Many of the pirates who surrendered had been wounded and died from their wounds within a few days.

Three pirate ships were still attacking. I fired some arrows at the nearest one, killing at least two pirates, one of them the helmsman. Those three ships broke away before we could do any major damage to them, leaving us for easier pickings. We shouted insults and kept firing arrows until they were out of range.

Our company sent a prize crew to board the captured pirate ship, along with several legionaries. The prize crew was made up of the *Mary Ann's* first mate Dirk Farwell, *Spring Flower's* second mate Alvan Ashman, and eight sailors. Their job was to sail the captured ship to the next port. The ship was worth a good amount of prize money, and it provided gold crowns for everyone in our company, including the soldiers, when we arrived at Cleopatra.

Chapter Five

For the next ten days, the weather wasfair, and the pirates were nowhere to be seen.I think out of fear of us, and for good reason.

We learned theTullianGeneral's name was Aulus Titius Longius. Hesaid he could useour help in defeating the new enemy thathadattacked the town of Cleopatra.Having seen what our wizards could do, he believed their power could easily inflict serious damage on the enemy's forces before they could launch an attack of their own.He offered a great deal of gold forour wizards to join his legion for the campaign against his new unknown enemy.

As we sailed into the port of Cleopatra, we sawa large lighthouse at the mouth of the harbor.

The town wason part of the delta of a river. To the east were hills thatwere part of the town's defenses. Allthe houses weremade from pink stones, with light gray roofs.We also sawseveral temples to gods we had never seen before. The temples looked different from the temples in Fair Haven or the ones I had seen in Winter Storm in the kingdom of Cynewyn.Through the open sides of the temples, I could see their gods' statues. Theystood ten feet high or higher, and manyof their gods had the body of a man or woman, but the head of an animal.

Some of the trees were also different from ones I knew.I learned that the one with large long leaves on the top and with no branches werecalledpalm trees.Other treeswerecalled olive trees.The temperaturewas hotter and drier than I had ever felt in my life.I preferred my home in the forest, which never grew hot, even in the summer, to here.

As wesailed into port, we were guided to an anchorage near one of Tullian's forts.We offloaded theTulliantroops and the captured pirates.Captain Fenwick asked for volunteers to help the Tullians for three weeks, saying they wouldreceive extra pay from the Tullians.I volunteered with the other two wizards, Ervin and Horton; three of our fivehealers; twenty fighters; and one of our translators.My uncle looked surprisedwhen I volunteered but said nothing.I was hoping to stretch my legs and map our journey.Mr. Blackwood was to lead us.I guessed he just wanted to stretch his land legs too.General Longius allowed us one day to prepare for the journey, and we all purchased extra waterskins and food.

The next day, the twenty-seven volunteers and what Tullians called theirlegion "Legio Duo"—whatever that meant in their language—left the town for the nearby foothills.That night we camped in one of the outlyingTullian forts.General Longius held a meeting in his tent with his officers and Bjorn Blackwood, and Mr. Blackwood described the meeting to the rest of us later.They had talked about how to use the spell casters in battle. Since General Longius had never used spell casters in his formation before, he asked how magic could be most effective against enemy troops and if it could interfere with the enemy's plans.For the remainder of the meeting, they worked out the tactics of battle.

About an hour and a half after the meeting began, I saw a few local women go into the tent with food.Shortly thereafter, we could hear music and laughter.Mr. Blackwood said that the entertainment was songs and stories from their history or about their gods.He was smiling as he told us this, and he seemed more relaxed.

We roseearly and set out for where the other Tulliangeneral and his men had fallen.We traveled for two days before we reached the battlefield, and it was a terrible sight.Decaying corpses still dressed in armor, broken weapons, and unit symbols shattered on the ground.Some of the dead looked like they'd been eaten by wild animals. General Longius ordered the burying of the Tullian dead, and there we establishedour night camp.General Longius sent out scouts, including Blackwood, to locate the enemy's trail.

After a half of a day, the scoutsfound the trail and returned to report. The enemy army had moved south toward some nearby villages.We followed their trail for three days, and we foundthree destroyed villages.Theyhad killed anyone who resisted and destroyed anything that they could not carry.

On the fourth day, we crested a small hill near the river and saw part of the enemy army.Itwas an army ofred-skinned goblins, about five hundred strong.It was camped in thefourth destroyed village.

After we set up camp, General Longius called for his officers to meet him in his tent.We had a cold camp that night, with no fires to give us away. He and his officers spent most of the night planning the attack for the next morning.We arose early and lined up in battle formation.Some of the Tullian troops, about twenty men, were to stay behind and guard our baggage train, which included twenty noncombatants, including the three young women who were General Longius's servants.

Those of us from the company—Mr. Blackwood, Ervin, Horton, the twenty sailors, and I—took our placesin the formation on the left side of the line.We were to act as an independent unit and support the legion where we could do the best. Along with General Longius, three Centurions were assigned to the right side.They were Aulus Palfurius, Gaius Fabius, and Titus Sextius, and each had been in the legion for at least twenty years and had fought in several campaigns.The other legionnaires were afraid of these men, who were known to always be in the center of a fight.When the signal was given, we moved quietly forward. *This seemed too easy,* I thought.Ervin and I looked around, and we saw anotherenemy force of men was moving up fromthe left sideofourformation.With General Longius on the right flank of the legion,he was unable to see what was coming.Ervin cast a magic spell ofmagical fire, the energy shaped like a ball, and cast itright into the middle of the enemy force.

"Form a Shield Wall," Mr. Blackwood shouted. "Arion! Keep me informed on what orders the Centurions are giving."

"Aye, Mr. Blackwood," Arion answered.

With Arion's report, we quickly learned what was happening. General Longius had seen Elvin's spell and the enemy's strategy. Changing his own plan, he ordered the left flank of his legion to attack the new force. He would lead the right flank on an attack of the enemy barricaded in the town.We were ordered to support his right-side force's attack with spells and arrows.

Our forces were able to join General Longius just as he approached the front line of red goblins thathad just formed a formation at the edge of the town.

As the battle began, Ervin, Horton, and I cast sleep spells that struck some of the goblins. The three Centurions—Aulus Palfurius, Gaius Fabius, and Titus Sextius—ordered their troops to throw their special spears. These spears bent after they struck a target, and so could not be thrown back. They threw two waves of these special spears. The spells and the spears left open holes in the red-skinned goblins' formation. Centurion Aulus Palfurius gave the order to attack, and in seconds, his men were in a sawtooth formation. They attacked with deadly effect, breaking through the goblins' line.

The legionnaires entered the town in a tight formation, cutting down the small groups of attacking goblins. The goblins attacked quickly, with no plan. They fought fearlessly, and their battle cries, full of insults and threats, could spark fear in the heart of any brave man. They spoke a version of goblin language my father had taught me, and I shuddered at some of their vile promises. They could not affect these legionnaires, though. Hundreds were killed.

Their leader was able to gather a large portion of his remaining troops, only to have Ervin cast another ball of fiery energy into the middle of his formation. Many of the goblins died, though the leader survived. Over half of his troops were not so lucky. He attempted to regroup his troops, but the legionnaires were on top of them. Centurion Aulus Palfurius's short sword cut down the leader as he attempted to escape.

Over three quarters of the enemy were left dead on the field of battle. We rescued many captured women and children. The remaining enemy was captured or killed, although a few escaped, dropping their weapons and shields and running like bats out of hell.

Once we destroyed the goblins' forces, we faced the Tullians' true enemy: human troops commanded by a man named Bezzi. General Bezzi had fought General Longius many times in the past and had vowed to wipe Tullians off the face of the world, but he didn't have the luck of his gods that day. His plan had been to use the red goblins to cut down many of the legionnaires before he threw his troops into battle. Instead, his plan was in shambles. His troops were in disarray after a few balls of magical energy struck them. He was not able to cope with the magic spells.

General Longius did not fail to press his advantage. In less than an hour, the Tullian forces had destroyed both armies. We had suffered casualties as well. From our company, we had lost one healer and ten men, which included Mr. Blackwood. Of the legionnaires, 256 men had died. Eighty-eight were wounded. On the other side, well over four hundred goblins had been killed and nearly as many human warriors.Bezzi was among their dead.The few survivors headed south.

General Longius was overjoyed by the victory.We buried our dead and then filled our sacks with treasures we recovered from the enemy dead. There wereivory elephants'tusks, silver coins, gold jewelry, and gems. General Longius ordered our camp to include a stockade.After the stockade was built and guards were at their posts, the general allowed his troops to eat and drink. Later that night, he held a small party for his officersand us.There were beer kegs, wine jugs, meat, bread, and entertainment. His three women served the food and drinks, and we ate and drank our fill.

"I never thought magic was so powerful," Centurion Aulus Palfurius said to Mr. Claymore, through Arion. "You and your whole company can cast magic?"

"No, only three of us can cast magic,"Mr.Noall said.

Claymore answered, "Miss Elizabeth Silverleaf, Mr. Horton Noall, and I are the only ones who know about magic."

"Can you teach anyone to cast magic?" Centurion Gaius Fabius asked.

Ervin laughed. "I can teach someone who has the ability to cast magic. However, keep in mind that the art is vanishingly small in our day, and that precious few elves, and even fewer men, have the gift to learn such things."

Centurion Titus Sextius leaned forward to ask, "How can you know if someone has the ability to cast?"

"There is a simple test I can do,"answered Mr. Claymore, "but I can't train more than two or three."

"Who are you training at this time?" Centurion Palfurius asked.

Ervin gestured to me. "Miss. Elizabeth Silverleaf here," stated Mr. Claymore."Her father began her training when she was young. I am working with her to finish her skillsso she can cast more powerful spells, like the energy of fire and lightning spells."

Centurion Fabius nodded. "I saw your Bess use a sword and bow in combat, but you had never used a sword."

"You're right, Mr. Noall and I can't use iron and steel weapons.But Bess's father taught her to use a sword and a bow.He was a Warcaster, which allows someone to use both iron weapons and magic spells in combat.There are only fewelves and very few humanswho can cast and swing a weapon at the same time," Mr. Claymore said.

"So, she is one of the very few humans that is a Warcaster?" Centurion Palfurius asked.

"No, I'm half elf," I said. "My father was a full wood elf."

A quieted moment ran over the party, then General Longius had been following our conversation, and he said to me, "I heard you are from a kingdom of Cynewyn."

"Aye, I'm from the town of Winter Storm in the kingdom of Cynewyn," I answered.

"Good! Then can you please sing some of the Cynewyn's songs and perform some of their dances for us?" General Longius said.

I looked at Mr. Claymore for approval. He nodded. "Aye, I can sing some of my people's songs," I answered the General.

I began singing some of the favored songs of my father. Luckily, some of our crew had brought their musical instruments, and they accompanied me on fiddle, hand drum, and flute.

When I was done, the three servant women sang and danced to songs that were General Longius's favorites.

We all enjoyed the party, and for a time, we forgot the ones we had lost in battle.

The General had sent beer and wine to all the legionnaires as a reward for their victory. Beyond the general's tent, we could hear them singing their own songs. By the time the general's party ended, all the legionnaires had fallen into a drunken sleep.

Chapter Six

T he next day, we headed south;after four days, wefinally came to a small walled town, whose name I had never heard before, nor couldpronounce.The town had been home to General Bezzi.General Longius sent a messenger into the town, informing them of the defeat of their army and orderingthem to surrender.Their answer was no.The Tullians were experienced warriors and were able to setup siege equipment rapidly.They cut down severalsurrounding trees and made catapults and huge crossbows that they called scorpions. With these deadly weapons, they began the siege.

The land where the town was located wasdry.There were about twenty wells around the town, and plants and trees grewnearthe wells.The town's walls, ten feet high and four feet thick, were made of bricks of dried mud.

Mr. Claymore, Mr. Noall, and I cast spells into the town every day until the town was taken.I used the casting to practice my more powerful spells. Even though they weren't as powerful as Ervin's, they caused damage and killed some of the defenders of the town manning the walls.I felt bad for the townsfolk, who wereunder attack for days.It reminded me of the time I helped defend Winter Storm from the dragon lich Berubazius.If they had surrendered in the beginning, many would not have died.But people don't like to be defeated and become slaves without a fight.

On the first day, thick black smoke rose over the walls from fires started by our spells.The smoke brought with it the smell of burning bodies. On that day,I cast my first ball of fiery energy shape. Though it was weak, I could tell it still caused some destruction.It would take time before I could cast more powerful spells equal to Ervin's.

After four days of barrages, we managed to knock a huge hole in part of the wall. General Longius ordered us to storm the town. As I climbed through the hole into the town, I saw that the town's troops had formed into battle formation near the break in the wall. They were lightly armored, protected only by leather and some scale armor. Ervin, Horton, and I dropped three balls of energy on them.Many of the enemy broke formation and ran for their lives.Other stood their ground, only to die as the legionnaires cut them down.The town of five thousand fell quickly.In this battle, our spells killed many and helped defeat the town.Two of our shipmates were killed; four were wounded.

With the defeat of the town, General Longius believed he had dealt a great blow to his enemy and released us from ouragreement.He was, however, able to persuade Mr.Horton Noallto join hiscampaign.

"I'm happy with the deal the General has offered," he said to Ervin and me."More money, better benefits, and I have a chance for a better life."

General Longius paid us what he owed us, twenty gold crowns each and part of the spoils.The next day,a Centurion in charge of eighty legionnaires, our group of eleven, and four hundred prisonersbegan to trek back to Cleopatra.It was a sad day as we left some of our comrades.

When we entered Cleopatra seven days later, the citizens lined the streets and cheered us. We marched on to the main barracks, where we were dismissed.We headed to the harbor to rejoin our company.Ervin and I met with all the captains to report on what had happened and how our party had fared.

The company had checkedaround to see when CaptainLac's company arrived at Cleopatra.They hadarrived and sailed two months ago.The Lac's company sailed west.

For our company, the loss of Bjorn Blackwood was a great blow.

Captain Hawking took it the hardest.He had lost the most from his crew, including Mr. Noall.

"We must turn back," Captain Hawking said as the captains all met to hear Ervin's and my report."We've lost the only man who has been to some of the kingdoms of the Far East."

Captain Dashwood shook his head. "Even though Mr. Blackwood is dead, we still have a good chance to make it to the Eastern Kingdom."

"You're wrong," Captain Hawking said. "We all will die."

My uncle raised his hand as if asking for peace. "We all stick together and hold our nerves. I believe we can make it to the great kingdoms of the Far East. We've lost a few key members of our company, but we still have a good chance to make it. We planned for loss."

"You all can go on," Captain Hawking said, "but I'm returning. My ship is damaged, and I can't repair her here. The *Raven* has a crack near the center of the keel."

"What about your crew?" my uncle asked. "Do not some want to go on?"

"I may have a few fools that want to go on, but I will not," Captain Hawking said.

"Then take anyone who wants to return to Fair Haven," Captain Dashwood said, "with our blessing."

The whole company was told that Captain Hawkins had decided to return to our home port of Fair Haven. He kept saying that it was because of the crack in the *Raven*'s keel and that he could not find the right type of wood in Cleopatra, but I believed he had simply lost his nerve. My uncle, though, said it was because he had lost too many friends and key members of his crew.

The *Raven* never made it back to Fair Haven. We only discovered this when we returned.

As we readied the ships to continue our journey, we checked to see when Captain Loc's company had arrived at Cleopatra. They had arrived and sailed two months earlier, and they had headed west.

The day we set sail west was warm and clear, with a few white clouds. We saluted the *Raven* and her crew as we sailed past them. The *Raven* and her remaining crew were preparing to join a convoy of twenty-one Tullian merchant ships headed back to the port of Tullian and then sail home.

For the next two days, the weather turned worse by the hour. By the third day, we were in our second major storm. The waves were at least ten feet high or more. Our captains and first mates had seen the storm coming and had prepared all four ships for it. The pump on *May's Rose* was working overtime as the waves washed the decks. We only had one sail set throughout the storm. Our luck held, though, for the storm was blowing in the direction we wanted to go and sped us on our way. Still, several lines snapped, and some sails were torn. On the four ships, five sailors were washed overboard, and we were able to recover only one. The other four were never seen again. The remaining crew was wet, and some were seasick from the storm. But we were in luck; on board the *May's Rose*, we didn't lose anyone.

On the sixth day out from Cleopatra, the skies cleared, and we were on course with a strong wind to our back. Later in the day, our lookout spotted an unusually large shark, about twenty feet long, swimming toward a pod of eleven dolphins. The shark attacked, viciously biting and wounding one of the dolphins. The other ten dolphins defended themselves, driving off the shark. Despite the gaping hole in its side, the wounded dolphin managed to swim off with the others. Some of the sailors took this to be a good omen. It was always considered lucky to see a dolphin swimming with a ship's wake.

The *Spring Flower's* lookout spotted a large island to the southwest an hour after we encountered the dolphins. The island was shown on the Tullian map we'd bought. The map indicated a small town on a bay on the west side of the island.

On its north and west coast, the island had towering cliffs with few trees on the top of them. Several small waterfalls poured from the top of the cliffs. We could see what might be beaches on the eastern side of the island, but we trusted the map and headed to the west side. As we sailed around the island, we saw several different seabirds, seals, and whales. To help extend our provisions, we caught some fish. They were huge, forty to fifty pounds each. I remember being happy to catch a two-pound fish.

When we reached the western side, we saw that the cliff ended at the mouth of the bay, which was marked by two tall stone lighthouses. Each of the lighthouses was built on a small rocky island, one on each side of the mouth of the bay. As we sailed between the two lighthouses, we could see their roofs had collapsed, indicating they had been abandoned for a long time. The mirrors used to signal ships were badly tarnished from the weather. This didn't set well with my uncle. He had us prepare for trouble. The other captains signaled that they were doing the same.

As we entered the bay, we found it empty of ships. The only things moving in it were some small whales and seals. The town looked like it could have held two thousand people. The town had eight stone piers, but there were no ships or boats. We tied up to one of the piers, and the captains organized landing parties from each ship. My uncle chose me to go with his party.

We walked south along the pier and saw five small merchant's ships that had sunk. We checked the pier's condition to see how long since it had last been used. By the weathering of the ropes, my uncle thought they had been installed about two months earlier. Captain Greenwood of the *Spring Flower* examined one of the ships. From its deterioration, he guessed it had sunk about two months ago as well. He could see large holes in its side.

His First mate, Kirk Mattock, gestured to the sailors with them. "Some of you men come with me to that stone building at the end of pier."

They entered the building with shields and weapons at the ready. "Check every room!" we heard Mr. Mattock shout, and the rest of us ran over.

As I entered the building, I saw dead bodies, the flesh already decomposing, covering the floor. It looked like the last stand of the town's residents and that no one had survived the battle. A few of the corpses had legionary armor and shields. One of bodies looked like a centurion, with his short sword covered with dried blood. His banded mail armor had been sliced open, as if a weapon could cut in three slices.

The *Spring Flower*'s Second Mate, Gibbon Hardwood, entered behind me. "You better stay out until we secure the building. There may be an ambush. We don't know who attacked this town."

"I'm not afraid," I said.

"You are one of our last wizards," Mr. Hardwood said. "Besides, I hate to lose your lovely face."

First Mate Mattock spotted me. "Miss Elizabeth, it's not safe for you to be here. Mr. Hardwood, get her out of here. Now!"

Within a half hour, the two-story stone building had been searched and setup as a defensible location for our company to fall back to if trouble showed up.

Captain Dashwood sent various groups to explore the rest of the town. We found that only a portion of the town's wall was made of stone, well built, with watchtowers every two hundred feet. The rest of the wall was made of wood and earth, and there were breaks in the wooden part of the wall on the southeastern side. Five of the town's buildings were two stories high and made of stones. The rest were made of wood, and half of them were partly burned. We found the town's wells and tested the water. It was safe to drink. We searched the town for any sign of life but found only dead bodies. We also found grains, jugs filled with olive oil and wine, jewelry, loose gemstones, and coins just lying around. There were some broken weapons, like spears, short swords, bows, arrows, and a Gyrlac-style long sword. I wondered what had happened to the town. What had attacked it? I also wondered if Loc's company had made it this far. Had they fought in the battle, or had they found the town abandoned too?

Although the town offered no chance to set up trading partners, we needed to stay for a short time in order to replenish our food and water supplies. We built a wall at the end of the pier as best we could and posted men atop it to stand guard.Our searchers saw the monstrous creatures of this island from the wall.Some walked on two legs, and others walked on four legs.One of the monsters looked like a big bird, taller than the tallest man, and another was a big cat with two long fangs.Other animals included elk, deer, bear, beaver, wolves, and different types of birds.

On the second day in the town, as we were repairing the wall, a flock of six of the enormous birds attacked us.We killed two of them and chased off the other four.That night we ate one of the two birds we killed.It was delicious and fed the whole company, with some meat leftover. The other was smoked for us to take on our journey.

We buried all the bodies we found, and though we never saw a living human, I could feel we were being watched.As for the weather, it was sunny in the morning and rained in the afternoon like clockwork. The air was hot and muggy all the time.

We stayed five days to resupply all the ships, hauling fresh water from the town's well and killed five of the big birds for their meat.Tullianum map showed that the island had three small villages as well. The captains decided we would explore them when we returned. For now, the company wanted to reach the Far Eastas soon as possible. We guessed that CaptainLoc's company was still ahead of us by two months.There had been no other signs they had visited this island other than the broken long sword. Since Captain Dashwood fearedLoc's company would block us from establishing any trade agreements in the eastern kingdoms, we wanted to sail on as quickly as we could.

We sailed west by northwest when we left the town. The morning was clear and bright.

Ervin and I believed we were two weeks from the next port in Kathy. Our guessproved to be right.Aftera week,our lookouts spotted people swimming in the water, and we lowered our ship's boat.We were able to save four Weisailors and a well-dressedold manwho was from Chin.They spoke a different language, and Ervin had to cast a language spell to speak with them.

The four Wei sailors were afraid of magic. But the old man understood magic and was not afraid of Ervin and I casting somespells.

They said their ship had been struck by a rogue wave. When I asked what that was, First Mate Hill explained.

"It's a huge wave that comes from nowhere and disappears without a trace. They were lucky. Usually there are no survivors."

The four sailors were able to help us to avoid different dangers in these waters, showing us wheretwo large reefs and seven hidden rockswere located.

The sailors were happy to return to their home port.The old man, named Mr. Chan Lee, was an Ambassador on a mission for the Emperor of Chin.He was following an ancient mapthat had been drawn over a hundred years ago. He asked a lot of questions about our last two ports, Tullian and Cleopatra. He asked about their government, military strength, religion, and people.He also asked about our homeland and people.I believed he did not know about the large island that lay between Cleopatra and his kingdom.

He wasinterested in elves as well, since there are no elves in Chin.

He made me nervous, so I kept myself away from him.I had a strange feeling he was hiding something from us.I, in turn, hid the fact that I was half elf.He did not need to know.I heard him askingthe crew a lot of questions about Elvin people.The crew told him about Elvin religions, magic, and ways of life, as they believed.Some of the facts were wrong.He seemed to be interested in anything dealing with elves.Whether out of want or need, I could not tell.

Mr. Lee also wanted to study our maps and ships' logs.We kept the master maps from him, but he did figure out that Mr. Claymore was the lead navigator of the company.He never found Elvin's or my maps, though.He did corner me on the quarterdeck once.

"I hear you speak elven," he said,"and know something about their religions and gods. I like to know about their religion and speak with them in their language.Can you help me?"

"I can, but I have little time to teach you," I said. "I'm learning to be a navigator, and it takes most of my time."

"You may not trust me, but I am not any danger to your elven friends," Mr. Lee said. "One of your shipmates said you know more about elfin culture than anyone onboard.I have a need for this knowledge and am willing to pay forit."

I decided to tell him half of the truth. "I have lived most of life in the elven kingdom of Cynewyn, and my father gave his life to protect it from danger," I said, "and I have many friends that are elves.I will give all I have to protect them."

"You are a true friend of elves," Mr. Lee said. "I will not push the issue at this time."

He turned and walked away and never asked me any more questions about elves.

Chapter Seven

Aweek after we picked up Mr. Lee and the sailors, our lookout spotted a land directly ahead. As we drew closer, I could see several hills and one large mountain. Our five guests recognized the hills and mountain, and the four Wei sailors guided us safely to Zhang, their homeport.

Zhang was well protected with two forts, one on either side of the entrance to the port.

We were able to find a good anchorage for our ships. Zhang was a large city; Mr. Lee said about twenty thousand people lived there. It was the largest city I had ever seen. The walls were thick and well made; their army looked well trained and well equipped. The harbor was filled with countless ships of different sizes. Mr. Lee told us they were called junks. The merchants of Zhang had rice, wheat, tea, silk, cotton, emerald, and spices for trade.

The Wei sailors had warned us that we would be viewed suspiciously in Zhang. We were watched, and controlled, by the Wei authorities who feared us. Most of the people of Zhang had never seen people as large as we were, and with our different-colored eyes and hair. They were afraid of us, but willing to trade with us. In fact, as soon as we disembarked, Wei soldiers accompanying a man in authority surrounded us.

Wei authorities asked us, "Do you have any elves in your company?"

"Our only full-blood elf died in battle near Cleopatra, two ports back," Captain Dashwood said."Why do you want to know about our elves?"

"We have beenorderedto bring any elves we find to the Emperor of Wei,"the man from port authority said. "The Emperor wantsto talk to all elves.They will be treated as guests of the Emperor."

Captain Dashwood hesitated and then said, "We do have two in our company who have lived with elves, but they are not full-blood elves."

The man from Port Authority spotted Chan Lee and bowed to him. "Ambassador Lee, please come with me. I will take you to see our Minister of Trade. I trust your mission to the Eastern Kingdom was successful?"

"Yes, I will follow you to yourMinister of Trade," Mr. Lee said, "but for my mission, I failed to reach the kingdom to the East."

With that, the two men left.

As for the four Wei sailors, they left as soon after we dropped anchor.We never saw them again.

Our merchants began trading with the merchants of Zhang. They asked the Zhang merchants about Chin. The Zhang merchants said that Chinwas an ally and hadseveralgood ports, but their best and largest port was the city of Po Hsien.

Mr. Irvin Ashman agreed to escort me through this great city.I think he liked me, and he kept me out of trouble.He acted like an older brother and kept our shipmates and strange men away from me.We tried the local food and entertainment.I kept my ears under my hair and never cast any spells in public. My uncle did allow us to sing and dance at night while we were in port.

The company had decided to return home.We had made it to one of the Eastern Kingdoms, and our cargo holds were filling with eastern goods. Though we had not explored the full eastern coast, we had found a port we could use as a base from which to explore farther in later journeys to the East.

As for Captain Loc's company, we heard nothing. I thought they did not make it to Zhang. They may have bypassed Zhang, but they would have needed supplies like water and food.

We had been in Zhang for a week whenMr. Lee returned, asking if he could talk with our ships' captains and merchants.The meeting was held onboard the *Mary Ann*.It lasted hours for the meeting, while most of us were busy loading cargo and preparing forour return journey to Fair Haven.

My uncletold me later that Mr. Lee wanted to sail to Po Hsien.He had received a letter from his emperor ordering him to return to Chin.The

Emperor Wei had some gifts for him to take to the Emperor of Chin, and he needed a fast ship to carry the gifts and his staff.

The next day, Mr. Lee returned with three servants and two bodyguards, and the four ships set sail once again.

For the first time in the voyage, I had to share my cabin with someone— one of Mr. Lee's female servants, Manako. She was a young woman, quite small and petite, with black hair and black eyes. Since Mr. Lee was sailing on the *Mary Ann*, I could not understand why Manako was sailing on the *May's Rose*. Perhaps it was because I was the only other woman in the company. In such close quarters, it was impossible for me to hide who I was. It didn't take her long to find out I was half elf and that I was able to read two different languages.

I had to cast a language spell so I could talk to her, and I learned some of her culture. She told me of an old woman who could tell the future. She had made a prediction to the Emperor of Chin. "There will be a year with three fire bolts in the night sky. After planting season, a young Elvin warrior will cause the death of a great warrior and destroy a great beast in a battle. These actions will save two great kingdoms from destruction."

The prediction confused me, and I asked her if Mr. Lee knew about it.

"Yes, he does," Manako answered. "He was sent to Tullian and Cleopatra to renew a treaty with them and find more information on elves. The old woman gave him a brief description of the elf, so he hopes to find him and bring him back."

"Did he tell you the description of the elf?" I asked.

"No. He is keeping that information to himself," she said.

"Why did he bring you along to go back to Chin?" I asked.

"I do not know why. I think he needs my service, since some of the other servants that went with him on his mission are dead."

"I need to go on watch now," I said, "but we can talk tomorrow."

"I have a question for you. Why did you not talk to me earlier if you can speak our language?" she asked me.

"That is easy. I cast a spell," I answered her. I went through the door to go to my watch.

"Maybe you can teach me Elvin," she said, "so we can talk without magic."

"If you teach me your language," I answered her.

We followed the coast north for twelve days before we reached Po Hsien. I talked to Manako every day to learn more about her culture and what to expect when we arrivedin Po Hsien.In return, I taught her about elven culture and language.

As we neared Po Hsien, we sailed past three other ports and saw a jumble of innumerable ships of different sizes and types.The route was well guarded, with a few warships to curtail pirates'activities.

When we reached Po Hsien, we were met by a harbormaster who guided us to our anchorage.We had to weave through more boats than I had ever seen in one place, all plying the harbor waters. The docks were full of people, loading and unloading merchandise from ships.Some of the streets leading away from the harbor were so full of people, I thought they were just a solid mass.Fromwhat I could see, most of the buildings were made of wood, standing four or five stories high.Twowere as high as seven stories.

We had to wait for customs to clear us to start trading in the city.In the meantime, we were able to send the Ambassador and his party to shore.

The next day, our whole company started to replace the ships'worn-out lines and sails.The *Spring Flower* was discovered to be in the worst shape.She was leaking badly andneeded work on her hull below the waterline.When customs finally arrived to inspect our ships and cargo, we asked if we could careen—that is, clean and repair the hull below the waterline—the *Spring Flower* in port.They said we could, but the shipyard could only do one of our ships at a time.

My uncle and the other ships' captains met on the *Mary Ann*. My uncle came back to inform the crew that all the ships would be careened. We were third in line.The careen would take two weeks per ship.The *Spring Flower*would be first, and the work would start in a week.

On the third day, we started to trade, selling our cargo and buying new trade goods and supplies.

Mr. Irvin Ashman again escorted me through the city, even though Mr. Gibbon Harwood—the second mate on *Spring Flower*—wanted to take me around the city.I suspected Mr. Ashman either wantedme for himself or to protect me from Mr. Harwood.As we walked around, checking out several different shops that carried silk dresses and unique jewelry, I was able to communicate with some of the words Manako had taught me.Many shops had different gems I never had seen before, and I learned they were called jade and rubies.We found a bathhouse with very hot water, with both men and women bathing together. Irvin's face turned red when he saw the men and women together in the tubswithout any clothes on.I think he'd been brought up to believe that men and women were not allowed to see each other's private parts unless they were man and wife. Or at least having sex.

Four days after we arrived in port, I was on anchor watch whenI saw Manako with three men, each bearing two swords in their sashes.She pointed at me and said something I could not hear.One of the men returned later to talk with my uncle and the other ships' captains.When he returned, my uncle told me that the man was Prince Edo Okyo, and he was the Ambassador of Ryujin.He had hired three of our ships to transport some iron ore, bolts of silk, blocks of greentea, and pieces of fine pottery to Ryujin's port of Izeki.

My uncle returned from the meeting and ordered part of our cargo to be stored in the warehouse our company had already rented forSpring Flower's cargo.It took three days to move part of our cargo, and then another four days to load Prince Okyo's special cargo.Prince Okyo and four other men, a type of warrior called samurai, would sail along with us on their larger ship called ajunk.

Chapter Eight

The *Mary Ann*, the *May's Rose*, the *Gwenfred*, and the junk set sail to Ryujin's port of Izeki on an overcast day, with a light rain falling. We estimated it would take a week to sail to Izeki with good weather. Though the sky kept looking like it would turn stormy, the weather held. We felt lucky.

We must have been following the tail end of a storm for five days. The last two days of our journey, we had clear skies and a good strong wind that allowed us to make five knots.

On the night before we reached Izeki, Mr. Hill said to me, "Ye finally received your sea legs, and the sea is getting into your blood, just like your uncle and me."

His words surprised me, but I decided he wanted to make me feel part of the crew, in the hopes I would stay with the ship after we return to Fair Haven.

"Aye, you are correct," I said. "And tomorrow we will be entering a new port with lots of new things to see."

Mr. Hill added, "Is ye watch is over? It is time for ye to get some sleep. Staying awake will not bring the morrow sooner. Get some sleep! We don't know what morrow will bring."

I said, "You're right. And I will need to be up in three hours for my next watch."

The next morning, I finished my watch one hour before we entered the port of Izeki, so I had time for breakfast. The hour passed slowly, until our lookout called an alarm because twenty ships and a red dragon were also heading toward the port. They were coming out of a fog southeast of us. The ships looked armed for war. My uncle called us to our battle stations.

I went below to put on my elfin chain shirt and then grabbed my father's sword, dagger, bow, and a dozen arrows. I returned to the main deck, where my uncle told me to go to the crow's nest. That would be my new battle station. He said he wanted to have a good archer and magic up high. I figured he wanted to keep me safe and not have both wizards in the same place.

We continued toward the Ryujin port fleet of twenty junks and the blood-red dragon with black markings and fifteen foot long. We were closing fast as the junks and the dragon as we were entering the port.

I had prepared only few assault spells, because I thought we were with one of their princes, no one would attack our company. I was wrong.

I learned later that the enemy's fleet was led by Asaka Hisoi, a samurai; his brother Asaka Gohei, a wizard; and a red dragon named Ryu Ishi. They attacked from two different directions: part of their army by a coast road and the other part by the sea. They believed they could defeat the local Daimyo named Izeki Kinsue and capture the town. The town was baited to lead the Shogun's army into a trap. The enemy Asaka Hisoi was a famous samurai who wanted to be Emperor of Ryujin.

His first part of the plan had worked by drawing most of the Daimyo Izeki Kinsue's forces to the coast road, but he failed to plan for any outside forces like us.

A portion of Asaka's fleet turned toward us, coming up on our starboard side, firing arrows at our ships as they closed in for the kill, or to drive us off. The red dragon saw us as well and attacked. It breathed fire on the *Mary Ann*, which was in the lead. We returned fire, with Ervin and me sending magic lightning energy bolts while our warriors let loose a flight of arrows. Glancing toward the *Mary Ann*, I saw that much of her crew had been killed or injured. Her steering may have damaged by the dragon's fire attack, for she aground on the rocky shores near the mouth of the harbor.

The dragon chose us as the next big threat to destroy. Ervin struck him with a second lightning energy bolt. The dragon responded by breathing fire on our main deck, instantly killing Mr. Ervin Claymore and many crew members.

"Hit that dammed dragon!Bess!" my uncle shouted up at me."Use your magic! Kill that dragon before he sinks us!"

I saw he was right. Only magic would kill the dragon. Our arrows and bolts were bouncing off his scales.

I cast all three of my magic energy bolts.The dragon was stunned for a second, and I shot my last arrow, hitting his right eye.It didn't faze him. He moved in closer, his head just under me, but I was out of arrows. As he prepared to breathe fire onto the main deck,I jumped onto his head with my father's sword in my hands.I struck him right between the eyes, driving my sword straight into his skull.He cried out and shook his head wildly, his cone of fire missing the *May's Rose*. He started to crash headfirst into the sea, and I leaped back onto the ship, grabbing the rigging and leaving my sword stuck in his head.

I scrambled down to the deck and grabbed one of my fallen shipmate's long sword and shield. When I looked back at the dragon, though, hewas not moving, just floating face down in the water.Believing the dragon was dead, I joined the battle on our main deck to push the enemyback off our ship. An enemy ship had come up on our starboard side, and their warriors had boarded the *May's Rose* as I fought the dragon.

My uncle was fighting a samurai. He struck hard and fast,his speed amazing, almost as fast as the best duelists in our company.My uncle fought him as best he could, as did the rest of our crew as they faced the samurai's troops.Our training with different weapons before we started the journey helpedus keep them from taking the ship.Mr. Ashman led five men to defend the forecastle, and I heard him laugh with joy as he fought.I started to follow him, when I saw my uncle was in trouble.

The samurai made a killing blow, but I blocked it with my shield.He looked at me in surprise and changed his focus to me.We danceda battle dance around, each other looking for the right time to strike alethal blow.His sword struck me numeroustimes but failed to penetrate my shirt Elvin chainmail. When he struck my helmet, the blow bounced off my head, butleft my ears ringing. I was able to shake off the effect and struckhim in thestomach at the same time, cutting him deeply.He fell to his knees. I slammed my shield into his helmeted head, sending him to the deck.Some of his men saw him fall and, thinking he was dead, and they had lost the battle, ran to save their lives.Others stayed as a rear guard, but the tide had turned in our favor. We killed all who remained with one exception, the samurai I had fought.I ordered Roland to bandage his wounds and secure him below until my uncle coulddecide what to do with him.Roland looked at me with anger in his eyes, but he obeyed me.

Upon removing my helmet, I foundthe samuraihadnearly cut through my helmet, and I had a wound on the left side of my head.Since the healer were busy with men more grievously wounded, I bandaged all my woundsthe best I could.Until I saw my blood, I felt no pain.I tried my best to control the pain, knowing I would need to learn how to do this if battle came again.

PrinceOkyocame aboard the *May's Rose*with his translator Fukuchi Sodan and several of his samurais.When Prince Okyo saw me with blood flowing down my face, he grabbed my armand forced me to sit down.

"I see you won the battle,"he said with a smile. "What of the samurai you fought? He was the leader of this attack. Did he escape?"

Isaid in a daze, "The enemy leader is in ironsbelow.I am sure our captains will agree to turn him over to the local Daimyoas a gift."As I spoke, I wondered if any of the captains still lived. A healer was tending to my uncle, but his wounds looked grievous.Ilooked into his eyes and said, "I hoped the local Daimyo Izeki Kinsue would allow us to trade in his town in return for his enemy."

Prince Edo Okyo just smiled at me.

I said, "I also hopedhe would allow me to bring all the remaining survivors of our company aboard the*May's Rose.*"

Ryujin Prince Edo Okyo said, "I agree to pass on yourrequests to Daimyo Izeki Kinsue."

I lifted my gaze and saw the*Mary Ann*had foundered on the rocks. *Gwenfred*was on its port side,sunk in shallow waters.The water was red from so many killed in battle.At least the *May's Rose*seemed to be in good-enough shape.

"Prepare to drop the anchor," I called."I think this was a good spot to anchor."Then I lowered myself to the deck to recover some strength.

The anchorage was away from the docks and shore.We would have a chance to prepare for battle if we needed to.

Afterwe dropped the anchor, Daimyo Izeki Kinsue's samurais arrived to see who had given them help.They boarded with one hand on their swords, ready to fight.I stood up, preparing for a new fight too.Upon seeing Prince Okyo, the samurais bowed and talked to him in his language.I shouted an order for my crew to put away their weapons, for these were friends. Then I told Roland to bring the enemy leader back on deck to give him to the Daimyo Izeki'stroops.

One of the Daimyo's samurais stepped up to me and offered me his right hand. I reached out with my right hand and grabbed his forearm. At that moment, Roland brought the wounded enemy leader onto the deck. As the daimyo's samurais drew their weapons again, I held the samurai's arm firmly. He looked surprised and angry, and I spoke to him through the prince's translator.

"The enemy leader is a gift to your Daimyo from our company." Then I released my grip on the samurai's arm.

He was stunned, but when he gathered his wits, he gave me a bear hug of joy and a smile. He understood I did not want another battle at this time.

The local Daimyo's samurai looked like they could not believe their luck as Roland turned over the enemy leader to them. They bowed to Prince Okyo and to me and my crew, and then they signaled for a nearby sampan to come alongside of the *May's Rose*. Within minutes, the enemy leader was in the sampan on his way to shore.

In the end, two-thirds of *May's Rose* crew had perished, including my uncle and the first mate. Their deaths, as well as those of my friends and shipmates, weighed heavily on me. I was the only ship officer of the *May's Rose* still alive. I might, I realized, be the only ship officer still alive from all three ships. Would this spell the failure of our adventure? So much responsibility, everyone's life depending on my actions—or lack of action.

I ordered Roland to take four men and the ship's longboat to see if anyone else was alive on the other ships. They had the longboat over the side and in the water in quick time, and they started to row to the *Mary Ann*.

Prince Okyo boarded another sampan, taking some of his samurais with him. They were heading to the city. He left two of his samurais and the translator on our ship. I assumed they were to keep anyone from our company from going to shore.

I asked, "Aldrich, can you retrieve my father's sword? I left it stuck in the head of the dragon."

"Aye, aye," Aldrich said.

I added, "Thank you."

As Aldrich went for my father's sword, I started bandaging our wounded. Aldrich also secured the body of the dragon.

Among the dead was my uncle, who had succumbed to his wounds. Mr. Hill had been burned to death by the dragon's fire. Irvin Ashman had been beheaded.

Ryujin warriors removed the enemy's dead as I and others who were capable wrapped our dead shipmates in canvas, preparing them for burial and last farewells. When we were done, I grabbed a bucket of water to wash my face and hands.

I ordered Aldrich to take charge of the anchor watch and to call out if someone came alongside. Then I went below to my uncle's cabin to write in the ship's log about the battle and enter the names of our honored dead. So many of our shipmates had died. We might never return home now.

By the time I finished the log entry, Roland had returned with six men from the *Mary Ann* and four from the *Gwenfred* who were fit for duty. Seven other men had serious wounds. I thought most of the wounded would not live out the night. Mr. Gibbon Harwood, the *Mary Ann*'s second mate, was among the wounded. We made the survivors as comfortable as we could.

Daimyo Izeki Kinsue sent word that he wanted to see the leader of our company at what he called a Head-reviewing ceremony.

I asked the translator what I needed to bring to the ceremony. The dragon's head perhaps?

"No," he answered. "People of Ryujin respect dragons. It would be bad manners to bring a dragon's head to the ceremony."

I thanked him for his advice and asked him to call for a boat to take us to shore. I would have to go without a head to show.

On the main deck, I addressed the crew. "I order you all not to leave the ship unless I call for you. Roland, break out a small keg of beer as a reward for the crew for its defense of our ships. Roland, I'm leaving you in command until I return."

"Miss Elizabeth, don't go," Roland said. "I fear that we will never see you again, and then who will command the ship back to Fair Haven? Please let me to go the ceremony in your place."

I patted him on his back in reassurance. "I will be back soon." At least my head had stopped pounding with pain.

A sampan had arrived to take us to the city. When Fukuchi Sodan and I stepped onto the beach, a samurai challenged us. I showed him the document from Daimyo Izeki. He bowed and ordered two samurais to escort us to the ceremony. They led us to a large tent near the northern gate of the castle.

All the samurais at the ceremony were still in their armor, so I was glad I had kept mine on. I was concerned that I still felt light-headed from my wounds and loss of blood. The others stared at me, maybe because I was female or maybe because they had never seen Elvin chain armor before.

Sodan quickly told me who some of the men facing me were. I of course recognized PrinceOkyo. He sat to the left of another Daimyo, Edo Tadao. Edo Tadao sat in the center, Sodan explained,because he was the Shogun, the top military commander. The local DaimyoIzeki Kinsuesat onShogun Edo Tadao's right.Ten more men satalong each side of the tent in two rows.

"What should I do to be polite and correct?"I askedFukuchi.

The translatorsaid, "Wait to be shown where you can sit, and say nothing unless asked."

I bowed to the three important leaders and waited to be seated.An armored warrior showed me to an empty chair near PrinceOkyo.Sodan sat behind me.

As Daimyo Izeki called out a name, a samurai stood up and brought forward the head of an enemy he said had been killed in battle. This was done until allthe Daimyo's samurais had presented their heads.

One of the samuraisshoutedsomething. I turned to Sodan, who told me the samurai had called for Asaka Hisoi.

As Asaka entered the tent, he saw me and shouted at me, "Ryuugoroshi!" I looked at him and bowed slightly. Many of the samurais were shouting at Asaka.

Daimyo Izeki spoke, and Sodan translated. "A Rose has brought us my enemy, Asaka Hisoi. Now what should I do with him?"

Again, everyone started talking. One of the samurais turned to me and spoke.

"He asks," Sodan said,"didyou kill the dragon?"

"Yes," I answered."I killed the red dragon for killing my company's leader, my ship's Captain, my shipmates, and a member of my family.Would you not have killed a dragon for killing your lord?"

After Sodan translated my words, the samurai shook his head and asked something else. Sodan told me he wanted to know what weapon I had used.

"I killed the dragon with my father's sword."Manako had told me some of the customs of Ryujin, and I pulled part of the blade out of its scabbard and then slammedit back in. "I also captured your lord's enemy alive and turned him over to Daimyo Izeki Kinsue."

A man in silk robes stepped out of the shadow. "I am Sakai Konyo," he said in Elvin. "Please let me see your sword."

I almost fainted from surprise, but I gave him my father's sword.

"Thissword was made byanElvin Master Sword Smith," he said in Elvin. He stepped closer and lifted my hair to see my ear. "And you are an elf!"

"My father waself, and my mother washuman," I said proudly.

"I see. You are a great warrior," he said and handed back my sword.

"I hope so. I live to honor my father's memory," I said with pride.

"I will have a doctor to attend to yourhead.Yourwound isstill bleeding." Sakai Konyocalled to another man at the back of the tent.

Sodan explained that this other man was a doctor, Akimoto Ukon. He led me to the side and looked at my bloody bandage, and thenhe removedit so he could see my wound better. Sodan translated what the doctor said to me, that it was a deep wound and he needed to clean it. I was to hold my head very still.

As the doctor cut my hair around the wound, Daimyo Izeki started to talk, and almost immediately others chimed in. Sodancould not translate what was being said becauseeveryone talked too fast.The doctor sewed up my wound, which hurt a lot, but I did not scream. I didn't want to offend the Prince or the two Daimyos.When he was done, he bandaged my head in fresh cloth and spoke to Sodan.

"The doctor believes you lost a lot of blood," Sodan said."You will need to rest for a few days."

"Youare right," I said,"but I have a lot to do.I think I need to ask for permission to leave and return to my ship."

All the talking had died down by that time, and samurais were leading Asaka Hisoi out of the tent. Heturned andyelled at me,and again Sodan translated,"At least I had a chance to fight a true warrior, unlike the ones who serveDaimyo Izeki Kinsue.She is the only one who can claim to have defeated me."

I kept quiet, not knowing what to say to Asaka Hisoi.After Asaka was out of the tent, I asked Sodan to ask Daimyo Izeki if I could return to my ship.

Sodanspoke, but it was the prince who answered.

"Prince Edo Okyo gives you permission to return to the ship," Sodan told me."The decision to allow you to sell your trade goods will be made in a day or two."

I told him to thank the prince for his time, and I stood up. I needed Sodan's help to stay up, weary from my wounds, loss of blood,and all the tragic losses of that day.Mr. Sodan helped me from the tent.Two samurais escorted us to a sampan, which took me to my ship.

Upon my return, I toldRoland I would be in my cabin and towake meonly if it was necessary.I repeated that no one was to go ashore without my permission.

"And I mean *no one!*" I repeated.

When I reached my cabin, I removed my armor and clothes, washed the blood off, put on a clean nightshirt, andcrawled into my bed.I fell asleep within minutes.

Next morning, I was rudely awakenedby someone knocking on the door of my cabin.

"I'm awake!" I yelled."Is it my watch now?" I was half asleep.

"No,Miss Elizabeth. Ye're not assigned a watch as ship's Captain, but ye are needed on deck.Two men are here to see ye."

I arose and dressed in my last clean shirt and pants.

I found Sakai Konyo and Doctor Akimoto Ukon on deck.Sakai Konyo wanted to study my father's sword and our wizard's spell book.He was offering Doctor Akimoto's servicesfor my crew in exchange.I took a few minutes to think about it and then agreed for the sake of the wounded crew.

I called Roland over to escort the doctor to our wounded, hoping he could save a few of them.

I led Konyo to my uncle's cabin so he would have a desk.As we passed my cabin, I took a moment to grab my sword from the peg it hung on.Inthe Captain's cabin, Idropped the sword on my uncle's desk,along with Ervin's book.

Leaving him to his studying, I returned to the main deck to see what repairs the *May's Rose* needed. As I reached the deck, I saw a sampan coming alongside with four samurais and Sodan in it.

They had come to inform me that Daimyo Izeki had agreed to allow us to salvage our cargo from the two sunken ships and to deliver the cargo Prince Okyo had contracted us to deliver to the port of Izeki.He was also willing to allow us to sell any of our goods to his people, but he would levy a tax of fifteenpercent of the cargo's value.We would be allowedto buy goods and supplies from his town.

I agreedafter a little haggling because I needed provisions for the return voyage.

Through Sodan, I asked one of the samurais to send a barge or some sampans to the *May's Rose* to offload PrinceOkyo's property.After agreeing, the samurai asked if I was willing to sell the dead dragon to the Daimyo.

"How much is the Daimyo willing to pay?" I asked.

"The Daimyo is willing to pay twenty Ch'ien for the dragon's body."

"Agreed," I said. "Plus, the right to bury our dead on one of the small islands at the mouth of the harbor."

He laughed and pointed to an island, and then said, *"Hi."* I already knew that word meant *yes*.

I turned to Roland. "Inform the crew that these men have just bought the dragon's body. Part of the price is land to bury our dead."

"Don't ye know how much a dragon's parts are worth?" Roland asked.

"Aye, but we need land to lay our fallen comrades to rest. Or do you think they don't deserve a grave?"

His look said it all. He was ashamed of what he had said. "I know you made this deal for the whole crew, not just for the living. I'm sorry for my words. Ye are right."

After the samurai took the dragon's body, I ordered Roland to take five men to the island to dig graves. "And I'm sorry for my words," I added.

"Aye, sir. Err, I mean, Miss Silverleaf."

After Roland and the others left, I went to check up on the doctor. He was busy with his nine patients—for all the wounded had lived through the night—but when he saw me, he came over to change my bandages.

Through Sodan, I found out the status of wounded crewmembers.

Mr. Gibbon Hardwood would recover, but Gavin and Selig were dying. The doctor could not prevent their deaths. He also said I needed to be in bed, resting from my wounds. I laughed and said I was the last ship officer standing. I would take it easy when I could.

According to the doctor's report, I had fifteen men fit for duty, including myself, and seven more available when they recovered. I planned for Mr. Gibbon to act as Captain of the *May's Rose* when he recovered. He'd had much more time on a ship than I, and I hoped he could handle the job.

I suddenly remembered Konyo. I had left him alone for over three hours. I was about to open the cabin's door when I heard a voice that was not Konyo's. I couldn't hear what was being said. I opened the door to find Konyo was the only person in the cabin. Where had the second voice come from?

"I have learned all I can for now," he said to me in Elvin.

"Where did the second voice come from?" I asked.

He laughed. "Well, your sword is magical."

"What? How did that happen?"

"The master sword smith was Elvin, and he knew magic."

"What kind of magic does it have? What are its powers?"

He said he needed more time to answer those questions. As he left the cabin, he added, "I will be back tomorrow to find the answers about your sword."

Hewalked down the hallway smiling and singing a song.

I felt I had got the worst part of the deal. Hehad got everything he wanted, and more.Oh, well. At least I had learned my sword was magical.But there was much more Ineeded to find out.

For the rest of the day,the crew worked on unloadingthe prince's property and our trade goods fromour hold, ferrying them to the town and storing them ina warehouse near the town's market. That night,I posted some sailors as guards on board.The Daimyo posted troops around the warehouse.

Early the next morning, Konyo returned so he could study my sword again. He brought Doctor Ukonalso. As the doctor again tended to the wounded, Konyo retreated to my uncle's cabin to study my sword. After two hours, hecalled for me.

"You are in danger from Asaka Gohei, the brother of Asaka Hisoi," he said as I walked into the cabin."Asaka Gohei is a wizard."

"How do you know this?" I asked.

"As you know, your sword is magical, but you do not know what magic it has.Your sword is aSoulStealer.The red dragon you killed;his soul is in the gem at the hilt of the sword. The brothers had planned a two-prong attack. Gohei was to lead ground forces and attack the town as Hisoi'sfleet entered the harbor.The plan was to divide the Daimyo's troops.If the Daimyo sent his samurais to repel Gohei's forces, then Hisoi's forces could land at the piers and sweep through the town.If the Daimyo sent his troops to repel Hosoi's forces,then Gohei would attack the Daimyo's troops from the rear. But they did not count on your company.Your men put up a good fight and kept Hosoi's men fighting on sea.As for the red dragon, hewas to hit and destroy the strongest point of the Daimyo's defenses.For the capture of his brother and the death of his dragon, Asaka Gohei willwant revenge against the Daimyo and you."

"Why have you told me this?" I asked.

"I hope by warning you, you can be prepared for his attack.As for your sword,are you willing to sell it? I'll pay a fair price."

"No. It was given to me by my father.It was his pride and joy.It has done me well in battle already.Now, about Gohei. Do you know when hewill attack me?"

"I know he left Ryujin after the battle.I don't know where he went." He started to leave the cabin, but then turned back."Ifyou ever change your mind, I would still like to acquire your sword."

After Konyo and the doctor returned to the town, I put Roland in charge of the ship and went ashore to start selling our cargo.We needed supplies for the return trip.

I was able to buy fresh fruits, rice wine, and dried fish. I also purchased new trade goods: fine red and black pottery, silk clothes, green tea, carved wood, and carved green jade.

When I returned to the ship, Rolandtold me the crew had askedhim to speak to me on their behalf.

"Mistress Elizabeth, we all want to go home.We are missing our wives and families.Our hold will soon be full of riches from the Far East, but we have lost many good men—friends and shipmates—and two of our ships.We fear we never will see home again if we don't go back soon.We know ye have no one to go back for, but we do.Please, can we all go home?"

"Mr. Roland, we are in agreement.We have been away from home too long."All members of the crew had reached the end of their endurance.This adventure could go no farther.

"Mr. Roland! Start preparing for the return voyage home. I will inform the Daimyo we are leaving after we complete our repairs and trade our goods for enough provisions,"I said.

The crew shouted for joy and jumped to prepare the ship for the journey home.

I had sent word by a local fisherman, whom I paid a silver coin, to have the translator meet me on the beach an hour after sunrise the next morning. I'd need him to go with me to see the Daimyo.After checking on the wounded, I brought the ship's log up to date.The Daimyo had purchasedallour iron, copper, and steel ingots, as well as half of the rest of our cargo.I was confident I had done well with my trading deals, getting enough supplies as well as valuable goods to trade. I had also located a mapmaker who was willing to sell some local maps to me under the table.Part of the price was that Iallowed him to copy some of my charts from our company's voyage.I hoped his charts were worth the price.

I returned to my cabin and I updated the log on the sales and purchases. When I finished the log entry, I went back on deck to join the crew, who were singing as they worked on readying the ship for sail. Weall sang and danced later, after darkness fell, until all but the watch went to bed.

The next day, I rose early to prepare to see the Daimyo.I washed and put on my best dress.I decided to leave my sword on board.

Sodan was there with two samurais, who escorted me to the Daimyo. He was pleased to see me and was overjoyed that I had decided to leave within a week. He had a gift for me: a long sword called akatana with three carved symbols on its blade. Sodan explained that thesymbolswere for their month of May, a Rose, and a friend. This was a sign to the Daimyo's friends and allies that I was his friend. The friends would show me respect when I showed them my sword. I thanked him. He smiled and said that I and my company had done more than could be expected even from a close friend. He added that he wouldpraythat we had a safe voyage home and hope that we returned soon. I bowed to him. As I left the room, I proudly carried the sword.

Ineightdays, we had repaired the battle damages and had packed the ship's hold with our provisions and new goods. I informed the crew that we would leave onthe morning tide. Mr. Gibbon Hardwood was still unfit for duty, soI had to remain in command of the *May's Rose* for the journey back to Po Hsien. I appointed Roland as first mate and Aldrich as second mate. From the *May's Rose* original crew, we had eight fit for duty. From the *Mary Ann*, nine had survived, and only six from the *Gwenfred*.

The next morning, we were under sail just as the sun rose over the hills of Ryujin. The sky was clear, and the wind was from the northeast. I saw the Chin junk was also raising anchor to join us for the return journeyto Po Hsien. On board were a few samurais, Sodan, and Prince Okyo. Both of our ships made good speed of about three knots. Though most of the crew were tired and sore, they moved quickly. They even jumped to needed tasks before I could utter a command. They were acting like they had a purpose and goal. The goal was home.

I found the job of ship's Captain to be the hardest I'd ever had. It was worse than the job of the pilot. As captain, you only sleep when you can. I had no watches, but I was on call all the time. Some nights I'd reach my bunk, only to be called back on deck to fix one problem or another. How did my uncle do this all the time and still love it? I now knew why I'd found my uncle asleep at his desk so often when he tried to eat his meals. I knew I would need to sleep for a week when we arrived at Po Hsien. My hat was off to all ships'Captains. They were worthy of respect.

Our journey took twelvedays, for the wind was against us and the sea was stormy. Mr. Gibbon Hardwood was not fit to take command until the day before we arrived at Po Hsien.

Chapter Nine

We waved to our comrades as we pulled up along *Springs Flower's* starboard side. As we dropped anchor, Captain Greenleaf boarded his longboat to come over, no doubt anxious to learn why only one ship had returned. As he boarded the *May's Rose*, I was sure he could see in Mr. Gibbon Hardwood's and my eyes what had happened.

"Well, Mr. Hardwood and Miss Silverleaf," he said, "I think we need to talk. To your cabin, Mr. Hardwood. Or is it yours, Miss Silverleaf?"

"It is my cabin," Gibbon answered. "Miss Elizabeth appointed me ship's Captain yesterday."

"Good," Captain Greenleaf said. "Then let us go below."

As we went below, Mr. Hardwood said, "Mr. Roland, I would be in my cabin, and inform me when the customs come alongside."

After we had entered the captain's cabin and closed the door, Captain Greenleaf immediately asked what had happened to the others.

"When we arrived at Izeki," I said, "the town was under attack from twenty or more ships. We went to their aid and were attacked in turn. We gave a good account of ourselves, but there were losses, some due to a dragon, the attacking force used against us. Both the *Mary Ann* and *Gwenfred* sank, and all the ships' officers were killed. We captured the enemy leaders and turned him over to the lord of Izeki. I was able to secure trade rights so we could refill our hold with provisions, and we set sail back here as soon as our repairs were complete, and the ship was seaworthy."

"These are tragic losses," Captain Greenleaf said, "but you both have shown good training by taking command at such young ages and bringing the ship to a safe harbor. However, I must propose that my firstmate take charge of the *May's Rose*. He has more experience of the sea and is ready to command his firstship."

"What will become of me?" Mr. Hardwood asked.

"Mr. Hardwood, you become first mate, while you, Miss Silverleaf, will assume the position of the *May's Rose*'s pilot," Captain Greenleaf said.

"What about the First mate onthe *Spring Flower*?" Mr. Hardwood asked.

"I will raise my Second mate to First mate because he'sstarting to know the sea. As for the lead navigator, Mr. Byam Appleton will assume thatposition. But Mr. Appleton never learned to make maps, so, Miss Silverleaf, since you have been trained as cartographer, you will continue making maps for the company."

"Aye, Captain," both Mr. Hardwood and I answered.

He looked away, an expression of sorrow crossing his face. "Did you bury your shipmates at sea?"

"No, weburied them on a small island I purchasedat the entrance to the port of Izeki, and we marked their graves."

Captain Greenleaf stated, "That is good. They were good sailors and shipmates. I thank you for them. On another matter, Miss Silverleaf, I need you to keep your ears covered until we leave. These people are still looking for elves for some reason, and I don't have a good feeling about it. Does anyone know you are part elf?"

I said, "Yes, Prince Edo Okyo of Ryujin, some of his samurais, Ambassador Lee, and his servant Manako. I believe they are looking for an elf because of a prophecy."

Captain Greenleaf shook his head. "This could be bad for us, and expressly for you. You are not to leave this ship until further notice. Do you know what the prophecy is?"

I nodded. "The prophecy says there will be a year with three fire bolts in the night sky. After planting seasons, a young elfin warrior will kill a great warrior and destroy a great beast in a battle. This will save two great kingdoms from destruction."

There was a knock on the door. When Captain Greenleaf called "Enter," Rolandopened the door. "Captain Hardwood, there are three city officials here to check the ship and cargo."

Captain Greenleaf told me to go to my cabin, and then he and Mr. Hardwood went topside to meet with the city officials.

They checked every part of the ship, including my cabin. They appeared to be looking for contraband material—weapons, forbidden books, and drugs. They took about an hour to check the ship. One of the inspectors did raise an eyebrow when my name was said. Gibbon told me that they had accounted for every weapon we had on board, but that as they were leaving, they seemed unimpressed with our ship and her cargo.

We spent the next eight days offloading the *May's Rose* so we could careen the ship's hull. During that time, we sold off most of our trade goods and acquired more: gems, bolts of silk, and spices. Roland mentioned to me that the city's streets seemed to be more crowded and busier than the last time we were there, but I did not think much about it.

On the ninth day, we started to careen the *May's Rose*. Her crew relocated to tents near a warehouse the company had rented to store our cargo. Captain Greenleaf, Captain Mattock, and I were summoned by the governor of the city to an audience with him the following day at noon.

I prepared for our meeting by putting on our best clothes. I wore a hat to cover my elfin ears and my forest-green dress with a gold design. I decided not to bring any weapons, other than a dagger, out of fear that it might be taken as a threat.

At eleven o'clock, I met Captain Greenleaf and Captain Mattock on a nearby boat landing. We all wondered why we had been summoned to appear before the Governor of the city. I could see why Captain Greenleaf and Captain Mattock had been asked to come, but me? I was a woman, and I knew the men in this culture looked down on women. We made our way to the city hall. After showing our summons to the guard at the front gate, he allowed Captain Greenleaf and Captain Mattock to proceed, but stopped me. Captain Greenleaf turned back and addressed the guard.

"The summons commanded all three of us by name to present ourselves to the governor. Now you say Miss Silverleaf can't present herself to the Governor. What should I inform him when he asks where Miss Silverleaf is? That you would not let her pass your post?"

The guard looked at the document again and ordered six soldiers to escort us to the governor. We were led to a large room and left there.

We waited for what seemed to be hours before the Governor arrived. With him was Prince Edo Okyo and a group of men. I recognized three of them from the head-reviewing ceremony after the battle at Izeki.

The Governor looked at me and said something in his language. A translator said to me, "Good, you're here. You will be part of my expedition, CaptainMay Rose."

I looked at Captain Greenleaf and Captain Mattock. Both looked stunned.

I turned back to the Governor. "I will do what I can, but Captain Greenleaf is now in command of our company, and I must obey his orders."

The Governor laughed and walked over to me.He lifted my hat, revealing my still-healing wound and my elf ears. He spoke again, and again the translator spoke.

The translator stated, "Good! You are the elf of prophecy. You are part of the expedition.Your lord must allow you to go."

The Governor spoke again, and the translator turned toCaptain Greenleaf. "Captain Greenleaf, you need to talk with our military advisor about her services for the Great Kingdom of Chin."

The translator, Captain Greenleaf, and another man walked over to a corner of the room to talk.

As if he feared some danger, Captain Mattock movedcloser to me, placing himself between me and the other men. With his hand on the hilt of his sword, he acted like a father protecting his daughter.

The Governor and the Prince were talking, and from the glances they kept sending me, I assumed they were talking about me.

In almost no time,Captain Greenleaf returned.His face said it all.

"Miss Silverleaf," he said in his commanding voice, "return to your quarters and prepare for a long journey.You will need your armor, weapons, and two weeks of rations."

Looking sad and frightened, he reached out and gave me a hug.He releasedme and turned to Captain Mattock. "Go with her and help her to prepare.It will be a dangerous journey, and I need her to return safe to us."

Captain Mattock asked, "I'll send some of our men to go with her."

Captain Greenleaf said, "That will not be necessary, they are sending a company of troops."

"Where is she meeting her party?"

Captain Greenleaf looked at the translator.

"At the landing docks near your ship, within two hours," he said.

Mr. Greenleaf yelled, "Captain Mattock, Miss Silverleaf, you have heard him."

We bothsaid, "Aye, aye,Captain," and left.

Upon returning to the tents near the warehouse, I gathered my belongings. I placed most of my belongings in my sea chest, including the katana, the long sword the Daimyoh ad given me. My adventure equipment I put in my backpack. I filled both of my water skins with water, and my wine skin with some of the last of elfin wine. All my scrolls went into a scroll case, and my spell book into my backpack. I put on my elfin chain mail and gathered my weapons: my father's sword, a main gauche, dagger, hand ax, short bow and twenty-four arrows, and a marline spike. I also packed my shield and helmet. I wrapped up Ervin's master map and handed the package to Mr. Hardwood to give to Captain Greenleaf.

"Just in case," I said, "I fail to return."

I walked out of my tent to find both crews waiting for me. They all said goodbye as fifty riders and a wagon approached the landing. I recognized four of them. They were three samurais who served Prince Okyo and Manako. I still didn't know who Manako really served.

Even to this day, I do not know.

At the front of the riders was a translator who introduced himself as Bau Yan. He also introduced the Chin officer beside him as Captain Wang Kagang.

"This horse is for you," Yan said, indicating a rider-less horse. "Can you ride?"

"Yes." With a leap, I mounted the horse with my backpack, weapons, and armor on. "Please lead the way we must go," I said to the captain. "I will follow."

He laughed and then shouted orders to the riders. They fell into formation. I was near the end of the column on the left, just in front of the wagon. As we headed for the northern city gate, the Chin soldiers began to sing. I think it was a war song, or maybe it was a lover's song. Whatever it was, it seemed to give them heart for what was ahead. As we rode through the city, residents gathered in the streets to watch. Many pointed at me, and I suspected they were there just to see an elf with reddish-brown hair and green eyes.

When we reached the gate, a guard stopped us. Captain Wang handed him a scroll. The guard looked at the scroll, bowed, and ordered the gate be opened. We passed through, traveling on to an unknown adventure.

Chapter Ten

W
e traveled about ten miles north that day, until we reached a small town, where we received food and lodging for the night.

Manako was assigned to my room. Again, we were the only women, and we could keep each other company. We went to our room to cleanup and change our clothes before supper. As we came down, the hall was full of noise until the crowd saw us. Then the place became deathly quiet. One man in particular was watching us. He had been talking with Captain Wang and his lead samurai, Fuse Daiki. Manako and I were led to a table where most of our party was already seated.

Yan, the translator, was there. He asked me what I liked to eat.

"What is good?" I asked.

He laughed. "Chicken and rice."

"Then that is what I will have." After he had ordered for me, I asked him, "Why are we here?"

He looked surprised. "We are to destroy a huge great undead dragon lich that has been destroying towns and villages north of here."

"What is his name?" I asked. I hoped it was Berubazius, the dragon lich that had killed my father.

"We don't know," Yan said. "Is it important?"

"No," I said. "I just would like to know."

After we all ate our supper, the Chin soldiers started to sing. After they had sung many of their songs, they asked me to sing one of my homeland's songs. I sung one of my father's favorite war songs. The soldiers seemed to enjoy it. Several urged me to sing more, when I heard someone walking behind me. I felt something just before he tried to stab a knife into my back, and I was able to dodge the blade. Whirling, I hit the assassin with a sleep spell, which knocked him out. He fell to the floor. The spell also affected a young barmaid, one of the Chin soldiers, and two bystanders.

Captain Wang was up in a flash, yelling at me. I really didn't need Yan to translate.

"Tell him," I said, "that this man tried to kill me. What do you expect me to do? Let him kill me?"

"You may kill the assassin to protect yourself," Captain Wang said. "But you may not kill one of my men and three bystanders too!"

"They are not dead."

I removed the assassin's belt, using it to tie him up. Then I walked over to the young Chin warrior and slapped him in the face to wake him up. I hit the young barmaid on the butt. As she woke up, she thought the warrior had hit her. She slapped his face. Boy, he was confused! His comrades laughed their heads off.

Captain Wang wasted no time in calling out orders to his men. Two of the soldiers grabbed the assassin, took away his weapons, and hauled him away. Everyone in our party put their armor on again. The near-death experience had sobered us up. I watched how much I drank until the end of this adventure. Someone wanted me dead. It could have been Asaka Gohei, wanting vengeance for his brother, or someone from Loc's company.

Next morning, we left early, just before sunrise. We had traveled northeast a few miles, when I rode up to Captain Wang, Yan accompanying me.

"Why and who wants me dead?" I asked.

"A Wu Jin—a wizard—named Asaka Gohei," the captain answered.

I nodded. "I killed his red dragon and turned over his brother to a local Ryujin Daimyo."

"I know," Captain Wang said. "Fuse Daiki already told me. Wu Jin Gohei plans to make a pact with a powerful man whose name the assassin does not know. He thinks this man is powerful enough and can help him with his plans to destroy the Ryujin Emperor. He wants to become the Emperor of Ryujin himself."

I knew I would have to face Asaka Gohei's someday, but for now, the dragonlich was a greater threat to me.

We traveled all day, stopping at each hamlet, village, and town we came across, asking for information about the undead dragon and Wu Jin Gohei. The more we learned, the more we had to change our direction. The undead dragon and Gohei were going in the same direction. Gohei was a day behind the dragon, and we were three days behind him. We had to march at night to catch up to them. We caught up to Wu Jin Gohei at a small town that had been destroyed by the undead dragon and was under the control of Wu Jin Gohei's small army.

Between the dragon's attack and the battle between the town's remaining soldiers and Gohei's forces, the countryside around the town was littered with bodies. One of the town's dead soldiers still held the town's flag at the main gate. It looked as though Gohei had lost many of his warriors. He had not set guards at the gate or on the walls, so we freely entered the town. The streets were full of bodies and broken weapons. Gohei and his remaining warriors were at the town's governor's palace.

As we stormed into the room where they had gathered, Gohei began to speak in the Chin language. The soldiers and samurais all looked confused and angry at him. He then turned to me and said in Elvin, "I will let you live, but you must turnover your sword to me. And you will live as my sex slave, or I will have no mercy on you or your men. Only you can save these men. Surrender or I'll take your sword off your dead body! Remember I am a great Wu Jin, and you are nothing but a barbarian warrior."

In my anger, I pulled my wand from my belt. "Then come and take it!" I said in Elvin. I used the last of the magic in the wand to hit him and three of his men with a lightning bolt. I killed the three men and badly wounded Gohei.

Captain Wang yelled out a command, and immediately his men drew their swords and attacked Gohei's warriors. I did the same, rushing to engage two of the enemy soldiers blocking my way to Gohei. I killed one with a single stroke and badly wounded the other. The other Chin soldiers were as successful in their fights, and we made quick work of Gohei's men.

Captain Wang walked up to Gohei and spoke to him. Yan translated for me.

"You said something that she disagreed with," Captain Wang said. "Rose is a Warrior Wu Jin, and wields great powers and sword, as you saw. As you know, she is hard to control. Next time, if there is a next time, do not underestimate her. Now, why do you want her sword?"

Gohei answered, but the only word I understood was "Berubazius." Judging by the samurais' expression, it was better that I did not know.

I spoke to Yan. "Berubazius is the dragonlich that killed my father a little over eightmonths ago."

The translator's face went white, and he quickly translated my words to CaptainWang and Fuse, the lead samurai. They both looked stunned, and then happy.

"Good!" Fuse said. "You know Berubazius. Now we have a fighting chance against the dragon."

"Only if he does not find out what our plan is," I said.

As the lead samurai Fuse was starting to pull out his sword, CaptainWang ordered twosoldiers to take Goheiaway. I never saw him again.

Later that day, we buried all the dead. Before supper, Captain Wang, Fuse, and I planned out our action for the next day. That night, after we made our wills, we all prepared for battle. Around the campfire, the men sang songs of love and lost love. The mood was soulful and sad.

The next morning, we marched to the spot that we had chosen to divide into three parties. I casta spell on my section so that we could speak the same language. Then we could work well together. We were the center section, and we would be the diversion during the battle so the other two sections could move in for the kill. My section was made of Samurai Abe Mito, a third ofChin warriors, and myself. The right section was led by Fuse Daiki, while Captain Wang led the left section. Manako and some wounded Chin warriors stayed back to guard the wagons with our supplies and belongings.

As we took our positions, the sun was just coming over the hills behind us. We could see the great dragon lich, forty-five feet long, with his bleached-white bones shiningthrough hisblood-red scales at different places around his body. He was curled up, resting. I hit him with a lightning bolt. The attack had begun! Just as the spell left my hands, something struck me from behind. Turning quickly, I saw a Chin soldier behind me, wielding his sword.

"There were two more attack forces behind you," he yelled to Berubazius.

His sword had not penetrated my back deeply, since I was protected by my elfin chainmail. I pulled out my main gauche and sword to defend myself. I attacked with a two-weapon fighting style, which caught him off guard. I used my sword to push his away as I brought the blade of my main gaucheinto his throat. Ashe fell to the ground, dead, I turned back to the battle.

Our force on Berubazius's right side hit him with a second bolt of lightning and a flight of arrows. He turned on them, blowing his breath of fire with such force, it shattered the cohesiveness of the group and killed.

I ran forward, shouting in Elvin, "Foolish Berubazius! I came all the way from Winter Storm to kill you, and now you waste your strength on a diversion."

Berubazius turned so quickly, I was caught off guard. He grabbed me with one clawed foot, pinning me to the ground. One of his claws pierced through my armor, slicing into my side. He lowered his great head to mine, his eyes fiery red. "No, you are the fool. That yellow gem on the hilt of your sword is part of my master's phylactery. Thank you for returning it to me. Fool!"

The force on the left was attacking with swords and spears, but Berubazius was fending them off with his tail.

One of the samurais, Abe Mito, avoided the lethal tail and struck Berubazius with all his strength. This shattered his katana sword, slivers of it flying everywhere. Still unable to move out from under the dragon's foot, I shouted at him, "Here, take my sword."

He grabbed the sword and struck Berubazius in the neck. The dragon swiveled his head around, jaws snapping, ready to bite Abe. Abe thrust my sword up into Berubazius's skull. The dragon convulsed, his entire body shaking. With a loud shattering sound, his bones fell away in all directions. As Abe pulled my sword out of the skull, the blade looked like it had shattered from within. Berubazius's voice came from the jewel in the sword's hilt, shouting in Elvin, "You cursed elf," he shouted in Elvin. "You tricked me! You made my master's phylactery into a prison!"

Abe looked angry and stunned that he had lost not only his katana, but my sword as well.

"We have trapped Berubazius and won the battle," I said. "This is a great day." I pushed the claw up and out of my side and my chain armor. It had taken under six minutes from the start of the battle to the destruction of Berubazius. We had lost seventeen Chin warriors, a Wu Jin, and a samurai, Fuse Daiki. His last action before his death was to give Abe his matching set of samurai swords. Abe was very thankful and bowed deeply to Mr. Fuse.

He turned to me, and I knew he was about to offer me the set, and I refused. "It would be smarter and better for you to keep them for the safety of all." His eyes showed thanks and understanding. "Besides," I went on, "a dragon usually has a great treasure, and we may find a greater sword. I have the first pick of the swords, if you agree."

He laughed and agreed to my offer.

After we buried our dead and cared for our wounded, we gathered twelve large sacks of the dragon's treasure. There were gold and silver coins, jade, jewelry, gems, weapons, and other valuable items.We placed the sacks in the wagons and started traveling back to Po Hsien.Another soldier and Ihad to ride in a wagon, since our wounds made us unable to stay on a horse.

On the return trip, residents of each town and village we passed throughwas eager to provide us with food and shelter at no cost.Everyone wanted to see the dragon'sskull and the victors.As before, they also wanted to stare at me. My different-colored hair and eyes seemed to delight them. Some were able to cut a lock of my hair. I was told it was considered a good luck charm.

The journey back to Po Hsien took twelvedays.I was able to ride the last two days.The soldier that had been in the wagon with me was not so lucky. He died three days from Po Hsien.

We divided the treasure into shares the night before we arrived at Po Hsien. My share was in a medium-size sack that felt light, even though it held one hundred gold coins, five hundred silver coins, three potions, a fine fur cloak, four silver goblets, a small jade statue of a horse, five lengths of silk, and a fine Elvin long sword with numerous small emeralds and rubies in its hilt.

When we reached Po Hsien's northern gate, the guard stopped us.When he checked the wagon that held the dragon's skull, his face turned pale. Captain Wang said something, and the guard jumped to attention and yelled for the gates to be opened wide. We headed directly for the Governor's palace. There we were led into the great hall.We brought the dragon's skull with us.

The Governor was holding court.Everyone fell silent as we entered the room.The Governor called us forward to see the dragon's skull, and then he spoke to the Captain.Captain Wang bowed to him and then gestured for his men to leave the room with him.

The Governortalked toOta Jiro and Abe Mito, and then they also bowed and walked over to Prince Okyo's side.Konyowas standing with the prince, and he smiled at me.

Manako and Yan, the translator, bowed to the Governor, so I did the same.The audience was over, and as I walked out of the room with Manako and Yan, Yan spoke to me.

"The Governor is overjoyed you completed his mission, but he knowsyou lost your magic sword duringthe battle.He would like to know what he can give you to replace it."

"I thank him," I said, "and know he has greater wisdom than I. What gift he gives will be proper and good." I spoke carefully hoping not to insult him and left the room before something else happened, or the governor asked me to do something else.

As I again tried to leave the room, Konyo walked up to us and said something in Chin to Yan then he spoke to me in Elvin. "Abe believes you are a samurai, and he still wants to give you his set of samurai swords to replace the sword you loaned to him in battle. But Prince Okyo needs him and his swords, so I offer a magical item that I will trade for the handle of your father's sword."

I was still grieving over the loss of my father's sword and was reluctant to give up the hilt. But I did not want to cause any bad blood between me and Chin and Ryujin.

"I must warn you," I said, "Berubazius's soul is in the yellow gem in the hilt of the sword."

I added, "Please tell Abe that I count him as a friend. To lose one's weapon in battle is bad, but it happened. For my sword, I feel its loss, but it did its job by helping us defeat Berubazius. I lay no blame on Abe. It is part of the life of a warrior. I know I can count on him for help. Tell him if he ever needs my help, he need only ask. As for your offer, I accept. But Berubazius will try to get free if he can." Then I handed him the remains of my sword.

Konyo smiled. "Yes, I know, but I can handle him. Abe is also willing to provide you any help if you are in need. Just ask. By the way, I have learned that your sword was a magic sword of Seven Soul Stealers." He brought out a silver necklace with a pendant of a dragon holding a small emerald gem in its claws. Placing it around my neck, he added, "May it protect you on your journeys through life." He handed me a piece of paper with words written on it. It read on the first line, *Ordaigh Athrach Chun Smaragaid Dragan,* and on the second line, *Faltas Chun Duine.*

As I walked out, Konyo called after me in a joking way, "You look terrible! You need rest. You also need to stop fighting dragons. They will kill you one day." Laughing, he walked to Prince Okyo.

As we walked into the hallway, both Manako and Yan said goodbye.

Manako hugged me, adding, "Thank you for your help and friendship. I owe you a favor."

"You're welcome. I believe you are a true friend, and I will call on you if I ever need your help."

I walked back to the boat landing our company had been using. When the crews of the *Spring Flower* and the *May's Rose* saw them, they all ran to me, grabbing and hugging me near to death. The *May's Rose* had just completed her careening. On the morrow'stide, she would be refloated.

Later that night, Captain Greenleaf and Captain Mattock came to my tent and asked if I felt up to resuming my duties as Pilot of *May's Rose*.

"Aye, I'm fit for duty," I answered.

"Good," Captain Mattock said. "But I'd like to know where Mr. Claymore's maps are. We need them for the return journey."

"I gave them to Captain Greenleaf for safekeeping before I left."

"Captain Greenleaf," Captain Mattock asked, "is this true?"

"She sent me Mr. Claymore's maps," Captain Greenleaf said in his commanding voice. "I have stored them in a safeplace. If anyone finds out where, we will lose both her and Claymore's maps to the Chin."

"That is a true statement," I said. "Mr. Claymore's master map is worth a fortune, but I have a copy of his map, and I have included Ryujin on it. Mr. Claymore warned me of the risk of being in prison for life because being on amap may place a kingdom in danger. A government may not want to take that risk."

"Then, Miss Silverleaf," Captain Greenleaf said, "keep your maps safe and out of sight."

As they left my tent, they wished me pleasant dreams.

The next morning, we refloated the *May's Rose* and started to fill her holds. The loading took five days. At night I worked on a paper copy of my map for the return voyage.

On the last day in port, Abe came with a package for me. It was a dress of dark green and red silk. I thanked him and told him to wait while I tried it on. I went down to my cabin and changed clothes.

When I returned with the new dress, his eyes sparkled with delight. He gave me a big hug and told me it looked great on me. "Do remember," he added, "that if you need a good sword, I am willing to provide it to you. Just ask."

As he was leaving, a messenger came with a scroll from the Governor of Po Hsien. It was a trading charter for our company to trade in Po Hsien for the next twenty years. It named Captain Greenleaf, Captain Mattock, and Captain Rose Silverleaf as officers of our company.

We estimated this trade charter was worth five times what we had in the holds of both ships put together.

Chapter Eleven

The next day we set sail to the port city of Zhang in the kingdom of Wei. Accompanying us were five junks. Two were larger than our ships, two were about the same size, and one was smaller. One of the larger junks carried Ambassador Chan Lee. Ambassador Lee had also brought one hundred Chin soldiers for protection from dangers and twelve servants. He never said what dangers he expected.

Though the day was overcast, it was mild. During the journey to Zhang, which took seventeen days, we sailed mostly with sunny days, with short periods of clouds and light rain. The shipping lanes were full of different types and sizes of ships going in all directions. The crew used the time to relearn the ropes, ship, and the sea.

When we reached Zhang, we found little had changed. The harbor and the city were still as busy, and we were led to the anchor site we'd had before. The city official inspected our ships and cargo. They were still looking for elves and had heard about my adventures with dragons and a famous samurai. They wondered why Captain Dashwood hadn't told them earlier about any half elves in the company. Still, they approved us to anchor and to trade with the city's traders. We traded some of our cargo for supplies from the many sampans in the harbor.

As news spread that I was on board, a great dragon slayer, boats started coming alongside so people could get a glimpse of me. When I went ashore to explore the city, I found walking through the streets difficult because so many people wanted to touch me. As before, some even tried to cut a lock of my hair to make a charm.

Two days after we arrived in port, I received a summons from the Emperor's court. I was to appear the next day, the hour after sunrise. I showed the document to Captain Mattock, and he conferred with Captain Greenleaf. Both were nervous about it and assigned three men to escort me to the Emperor. I believed it was imperative that I convince the Emperor that I was an unimportant woman, not a danger to his kingdom. I also didn't want him to know that I was a cartographer. He might want to keep me as a prisoner in his court, either because I was half elf or a cartographer.

I dressed in one of my best dresses and armed myself only with my magic spells. The three crewmembers and I were met by eight palace guards at the boat landing. The guards escorted us through the city, crowded with its citizens, to the palace. When we arrived, my three escorts were stopped and told to wait at the gate. I was escorted to the Emperor alone.

He was sitting for breakfast in an open meeting room and had ten beautiful women servants surrounding him. He was short by our standards and looked about sixty years old.

As I entered the room, I was checked for weapons before I was escorted to the table. I was told to sit to the right of the Emperor.

He poured a cup of hot tea for me. "Do you know of the prediction about a great Elvin warrior?" he asked.

I picked up the cup. "I heard about it, and I know many believe it is about me. I fought one young red dragon with the help of my ship's crew. I killed the red dragon and captured his master, who was one of the enemy leaders in the battle at a port in Ryujin."

The Emperor smiled as he passed a noodle dish to me. "Yes, that sounds like one of the predictions of the deeds by the hero elf. You did save the kingdom of Ryujin from a great danger and destruction."

"Yes, but we did not plan to save Ryujin. It just happened."

"I see. So you don't see yourself as the elf of the prediction?"

"I do not."

"And yet you fought another dragon."

"I did. I fought with fifty Chin soldiers against a dragon lich named Berubazius. Some say I saved both the kingdoms of Ryujin and Chin, but I had help in both battles. Most of the men who fought by my side were good warriors, and in both these battles, many good men lost their lives."

"More tea?" the Emperor asked.

"Thank you. I will take some more of this good tea."

The Emperor poured the tea. "I believe you are the great elfin warrior of the prediction."

"If this great Elvin warrior was supposed to save two kingdoms with the help of sailors and warriors, then, yes, I am that warrior."

The Emperor smiled. "Good. Then I would like you to live in my palace as my guest to protect my kingdom!"

"Emperor of Wei," I answered quickly, "I have saved two kingdoms as the prediction said. But the prediction did not say three kingdoms. If you hold me here so I can protect your kingdom, it could be a disaster for you and me."

"What? Are you saying I am making a mistake?"

"No, you are not making a mistake. But someone may have misinformed you. I was predicted to save only two kingdoms. This means your kingdom is not in danger, and it would be unwise to keep me. Is this not true?"

His relief was clear on his face, and he started a new set of questions. "Why are you part of your company?"

I answered him, "My uncle had no one he trusted to leave me with, and he liked my cooking."

He asked me, "So you are their cook and nothing else?"

I laughed. "My mother taught me to cook and sew, my father taught me the ways of a warrior. Most men fight with a sword better than me, but I am still good at cooking deer and boar. My uncle tried to teach me of the sea and navigation. I still have a lot of learn before I'm an adequate sailor."

"I would like you to stay with me," the emperor said again. "My prime minister believes you are this kingdom's protector. He has informed me that there is a great danger that you will deal with, and thereby protect my kingdom."

"I need to return home, so I'm declining your offer," I said.

A well-dressed man and an old woman came into the room and walked up to the table. They both knelt and bowed their heads to the floor. The Emperor told me that man was the prime minister of Wei; the old woman was the one who had made the prediction of the great elven warrior.

"My Emperor and the elf protector," the prime minister said, still kneeling, "I need to inform you that I am going to kill you both and place your younger son on the throne."As he stood, he called out, "My soldiers, enter and kill the Emperor and this elf!"

The old woman looked at the prime minister and started to laugh. Then she looked at me and said, "I'm sorry, my lady."She yelled, *"Ordaigh Athrach Chun Smaragaid Dragan!"*

As the prime minister's troops entered the room, I beganto feel strange, as if my body was lengthening and expanding.My dress split, and the Emperor stared at me with eyes full of fear. The soldiers stopped in their tracks. When I stopped changing, my dress lay in pieces on the floor. I turned to see my reflection in the large bronze gong behind the Emperor. I was a dragon, a dragon with emerald-colored scales and leather wings.

I whirled back around as I saw the prime minister move. He grabbed a sword and stabbed the old woman. "You witch!" he shouted at her. "You will not live to release any more spells to stop me. As for you,elven warrior, you are dead!"

He signaled to his soldiers, and one rushed forward to attack me.

"We, the men of Winter Strom, to arms!"I shouted my father's battle cry as I swung my right front leg at the man.I hit him, and he went flying out one of the windows.

"Killthe dragon!" the prime minister yelled."We must defeat her before shebreathes on us."

I swung at him, my claws missing him by inches. Realizing he was my target, he froze with fear.Most of his men dropped their weaponsand ran. Those that were not afraid attacked, rushing at me all at once. I quickly moved to guard myself with my front legs and tail. Intent on attacking me, the prime minister's soldiers didn't notice the Emperor's loyal troops rushing into the room.They attacked from the rear, and soon the prime minister's men were all killed. I turned to the old woman and picked her up carefully.

"I'm sorry," she said,"but I had to stop him and did not know what else to do.Forgive me?I had to reveal your greatest power that you had hidden from the world."

"You cost me my dress," I said,"and now when I change back, I will have nothing to wear." I laughed. "I forgive you.But next time, let me know you're going change me.I would have brought another dress to wear."

The Emperor called to one of his servants, "Bring her a dress to wear."

As the woman left the room, he turned to me. "You are greater than you said.Was it to protect me and my kingdom?"

"With great power comes great dangers," I said,"and I must protect others."

When the servant returned with a dress, I said, *"Faltas Chun Duine."*

I changed back to myself and dressed quickly.One of the servants brought a mirror. I had to admit, the delicate pink of the silk gown complemented my reddish-brown hair. I admired the beautiful brocade work in blue of dragons and phoenixes on one of the wide, loose-fitting sleeves. The sleeves were the only thing about the dress that could be called*loose-fitting.* Either Wei women were even smaller than I'd thought, or I was eating very wellon this voyage.

I turned to the Emperor. "With your permission, I would like to return to my comrades at the gate.I also ask that what happened here is not known outside these walls.Please."

The Emperor smiled. "Yes, go with my blessing. Continue your journey and safe voyage home.I will not let it be known."

I returnedto my three crewmembers at the gate, with twelve soldiersas escorts.

"What happened in the meeting with the Emperor?" they asked."We heard alarms and shouts inside the walls. And why didyou change your dress?"

"The Emperor and I were talking about my adventures at Ryujin and with the dragon lich, and his soldiers got a bit excited with the tales.And the Emperorgave me this gown as a gift. It's a little bit tight on me, don't you think?"

As we walked back toward the quay, the three of them exchanged looks and whispered, and I heard one of them utter in an embarrassed tone, "Lads, better we don't say nothing."I suppressed a chuckle.

Aswe walked up the *May's Rose* gangway, Isaw Mr. Lee,a translator, and his ship'sCaptainand navigator.I secretly cast a language spell so that I could listen in on any conversations they held among themselves. As I reached Mr. Lee, Captain Mattock joined us.

Mr. Leegreeted me through his translator,adding that he admired my new dress. So, apparently, did the Captain and Navigator. They both stared at me with hungry eyes.

"I would like to acquire an updated map to the portsof Cleopatra and Tullian," Mr. Lee went on.

I nodded in reply, a little red in the face. "The dress was a gift from the Wei Emperor.It is a bit small for me.As for the updated map of Cleopatra and Tullian, I will need to talk to the company's actingcartographer.He may want some local maps of Chin or Wei, and some crown gold coins, in payment. Are you willing to provide some maps of Chin or Wei?"

Mr. Lee looked at his ship's navigator and captain. "Can we provide some navigational maps of Wei and Chin?" he asked them in their language.

"We have some navigation maps," the navigator nervously answered, "and we do need to acquire new maps for the journey to Cleopatra and Tullian. But our maps could be used against Chin, and so the Emperor of Chin forbids any other empires from acquiring them. We could provide a few navigational maps of Wei."

Mr. Lee turned back to me and spoke through his translator. "We offer a few maps of Wei. Is this acceptable to your company's cartographer? But I thought Mr. Claymore was your company's cartographer? He died at Ryujin, didn't he?"

The navigator spoke again to Mr. Lee in their language. "They have a cartographer in their company. Why I was not told?"

"I have my reason," Mr. Lee said angrily. "I still need those updated maps, so be quiet."

I looked at Captain Mattock and then answered Mr. Lee through the translator. "Yes, Mr. Claymore died at Ryujin, and he was acting as our cartographer, but he was not a trained cartographer. Our company has someone who can make you a copy of the maps of Cleopatra and Tullian. I will pass on to that person your request and your offer of navigational maps of Wei."

Mr. Lee shook his head. "I would like to make the offer in person to the one who has the maps. Please provide his name to me."

Captain Mattock stepped in. "I'm sorry, but I cannot allow that. Our company wants to keep his name a secret. Miss Elizabeth, you need to return to your duties."

"Aye, sir," I said, but I walked away slowly enough that I could hear their continuing conversation.

Mr. Lee said to Captain Mattock, "I hear that Mr. Claymore kept a map of your company's journey. I would like to buy that map if I could for the Empire of Chin. Could you name the price for his map?"

"I cannot help you," Captain Mattock said. "I don't know what happened to any of Mr. Claymore's maps. The one who has those maps has them well hidden, and he may not want to sell them to you. He can make a good life for himself and his family by selling copies of those maps himself."

"I am sorry," Mr. Lee said, "to hear your company consider those maps so very valuable and you are not willing to sell them to me."

"We will have the mapsyou requested made in a few days.Please have the payment ready when we deliver them to you."

Mr. Lee bowed. "Thank you,Captain Mattock, for the maps."He and the others departed the *May's Rose*.

We spent five days sellingsome of our cargo and restocking the ship.I finished the maps for Mr. Lee in four days and sent them to him through Captain Mattock.During that time, both the captain and I felt like we were being watched.Several times we thought someone had boarded the ship and left before he was discovered by anyone.

The day we left,accompanied by the two large junks that had traveled with us from Po Hsien,was heavily overcastwith rain.The harbormaster reported a major storm by nightfall.He was right.We hit the storm that night when we were twenty-five miles from shore.The storm lasted for six days.We madelittle headway until it had passed.Although the junks were better designed for stormy weather, their crews were not as skilled as ours.We were forced to replace two of our sails during the storm, and three men were nearly lost.

Chapter Twelve

I was on watch two days after the storm, when I saw a start of a rogue wave. It was about five miles ahead of our bow. It started as a small wave that joined other waves, growing to an enormous height, taller than our mast. The rogue wave moved very fast. Luckily it was traveling in the direction as we were, and in minutes, it was gone.

The rest of the voyage was uneventful. It took us twenty days to make it to the island where we had found the ghost town. The sky was partly cloudy, and the weather was muggy, although it was not hot.

From a distance, the ghost town appeared to be unchanged, but we felt something was wrong. As we approached, we found a partly sunk Tullian ship at the dock and several bodies near or on the ship.

The captains of all four ships called for their crews to prepare for battle. The *Spring Flower* sailed slowly to the dock, followed closely by one of the junks. As both ships docked, armed troops raced down onto the dock to guard the ships, but no one came to attack them. After the *May's Rose* and the other junk docked, the captains ordered some of their crews to stay on deck to guard the ships while others joined the first group on the dock. Captain Greenleaf ordered several of us to explore to the closest building—a two-story stone building with the doors barred from the inside. Two men busted the door down, and we found two survivors in the building. Our translator

Hektor spoke with them and told us what they said. One man's name was Mr.Quintus Atius Remus. The other was Senator Titus Claudius Romulus.

I remembered one of those names from something I'd read before. I tried to remember what.

"Our ship arrived here at this island yesterday," the senator said. "Last night we were attacked by many short humanoid creatures.They stood about three feet high, walking on their hind legs like men. They looked like lizards with small wings. They are obviously intelligent, for they attacked us with military planning."

Searching the town, we found various weapons made with stones: small spears, hand axes, and arrowheads.We also found three-toed footprintsall over the streets. We also found them at two spots just outside the walls.I believed thiswas where they had entered the town.

Among the bodies of the dead were five men dressed in clothes that were common in Gyrlac. Their armor and weapons were also of Gyrlac design. They could have come from Loc's Company. If they had made it to this island, theycould have established a settlement somewhere. Or they were shipwrecked.

Through Hektor, I asked the two men from Tullian if they knew the five strangely dressed men.

"These five men were in the town when we arrived," Senator Romulus said. "They could not speak our language.They indicated they needed help and wanted us to go to the other side of the island."

I talkedto Captain Greenleaf and Captain Mattock what I'd learned.

"I wonderif we should sail around the island," I added,"to see if Loc's company needs help, and see if his two ships have sunk or if their crews are still alive."

"Ihave fought Captain Loc before," Captain Greenleaf said."He was one of Gyrlac's best fighters, and I found him to be a very skilled and knowledgeable seaman.If he is still alive,it would be worth a small fortune to rescue him."

Captain Matlock nodded. "I agree that we should sail around the island to see if any of Loc's crew has survived, but I don't have much hope."

"Then we agree," Captain Greenleaf said."We will sail around the island tomorrow morning and see if we can give aid to Loc's company."

We set sail the next day, with the *May's Rose* sailingnorth and *the Spring Flower*sailing south. We figuredwewould meet up on the other side of the island in about three days.

As the navigator of the *May's Rose*, I mapped the outline of the island as we sailed. From the deck, we spotted many new plants and animals as we traveled along.

Around noon on the second day, we sailed around a hill that stuck out from the island. Beyond it, we found a large shallow baywith two wrecked ships. One was a carrack lying on her starboard side, half sunk. The other was acaravel, broken in half, near the beach.

We anchored a half mile off the beach.Captain Mattock had our longboat lowered and told.Mr. Hardwood led a party ashore.We all watched from the deck as they explored the beach. Just inside the tree line, they found a wooden stockade and several small huts. Inside two of the huts weresix men from the doomed expedition. All were half-starved and close to death. Among them was Captain Rowen Loc.He was a broken man with his lower right leg missing.

When Captain Loc was carried onto the *May's Rose*, Captain Mattock welcomed him aboard.

"Where is Captain Fenwick?" Captain Loc asked."Is he not the master of this ship?"

"No," Captain Mattock answered."I command the *May's Rose*.Captain Fenwick died in battle in Ryujin.His heir is with us, Miss ElizabethRose Silverleaf. Miss Silverleaf has been our navigator for the journey home."

Captain Loc looked puzzled. "He allowed a woman to be part of his crew?And you made her the navigator?I thought Mr. Claymore was the ship's pilot. And you were the first mate of the *Spring Flower*, weren't you?"

"Aye, I was. With the death of Captain Fenwick and his first mate, I took command of the *May's Rose*.As for Miss Elizabeth, shecame to live with Captain Fenwick after her father died.Captain Fenwick had no one to leave her with, so he brought her on this journey. He had Mr. Claymore train her to be a navigator and a wizard.She had proven herself in a number of battles and commanded the *May's Rose*herself for over a week."

Captain Loc turned to me. "So, Miss Elizabeth, you're a navigator and wizard?Does the crew respect you and obey your commands?"

"Ask the crew," I answered."They have obeyed my orders so far.Would you like some soup and bread?"

"I thought you would never ask!"Captain Loc said.

We fed him and the other men, and they all ate as if they had not seen food in weeks.

"Did you know we found the *Zaria* wrecked on a reef?" I asked the captain when he was done eating. "She had no survivors onboard."

"She was a good ship and had one of the best captains I have ever known," he said.

Our lookout in the crow's nest called out, "There are sails off to the north. She is coming fast. She looks like the *Spring Flower*."

"If it is the *Spring Flower*," Captain Loc said, "then she is commanded by Captain Greenleaf."

Remembering what Captain Greenleaf had said about Captain Loc, I asked, "Do you know Captain Greenleaf?"

Captain Loc nodded. "Aye. He and Captain Mattock killed my second son in a battle just off Gyrlac. They took my son's ship and her cargo. They used the money from selling the ship and cargo to buy the *Spring Flower*."

I felt sorry for him and did not ask any more questions about his relationship with Captain Greenleaf and Captain Mattock. "I need to return to my duties," I said. "I'll talk to you later."

Captain Loc nodded. "Thank you for food and your help."

Not long after, Captain Mattock sought me out and handed me three large books. "Can you take these books below and find a safe place for them?"

"Aye, sir." The books were the ships' logs from the two remaining ships from Captain Loc's expedition and the navigator's book.

After the *Spring Flower* arrived in the bay, we raised anchor and set sail back to the port on the other side of the island. We could see a storm brewing to the northeast of the island and wanted to make it back to the harbor as quickly as possible. We set every bit of sails we could and were able to make five knots heading south with the wind behind us. Captain Mattock ordered the hatches to be batten down. We sailed out from the island because of the reefs we had found during the voyage of the last two days.

The rain started at dusk. I figured it would be sunset tomorrow before we made it around the southern point of the island. The weather became worse with each passing hour. Both ships rounded the southern point about dusk the next day.

With the island between us and the storm, the waves were not as bad as they had been on the eastern side of the island. As we tacked, heading north to the ghost town, the rain poured down in sheets of water and the chop grew heavy, the waves growing. Everyone on deck was soaked to the bone. It took us another day of fighting the weather to make it to the mouth of the harbor. We sailed straight to the pier and tied up with double the normal lines. There we were safe from the worst of the storm. We could see the waves were huge just beyond the bay. Some of the waves even broke over the harbor's break wall. The storm was full of lightning and thunder.

Once the ship was safely tied to the pier, I was no longer required to be on deck and went to my cabin. As I lay on my bunk, I read the other ships' logbooks. I read about the Loc's expedition's adventures, which included the last storm they ran into, which damaged both ships before they could make it to the sheltered bay where we'd found them.

Both ships lost most of their crew and supplies to the storm. Twenty-one survivors made it to shore, but many were injured, including Captain Loc.

The next day, they built the stockade and few huts for shelter. For Captain Loc, after four days, his leg became infected so badly, they had to cut it off just below the knee to save his life. Six days after their landing, they sent four men to try to reach a town they believed was on the other side of the island. They were never heard from again. Twenty days later, they sent seven more men to find help. They were never heard from either. Captain Loc concluded in the log that the island was full of many dangers.

Earlier in the logbook, I read that both Mr. Remus and Senator Romulus had met and made deals with Captain Loc when his company was in the port City of Tullian.

The storm lasted for two more days before it blew itself out. We hunted some big birds for food to take on our journey to Cleopatra. The hunting was good, and we killed three birds. Captain Loc and two of his crew said they did not want to sail with a woman. They believed it was bad luck, so they were transferred to the *Spring Flower*. One of the sailors made Captain Loc a peg leg so he could walk the deck of the *Spring Flower*.

Ambassador Chan Lee decided to leave sixty of his soldiers and one of his junks to control the town for Chin. I warned him that small lizard men lived on the island and they might not like him leaving soldiers in town. These lizard men could think and were able to fight.

He laughed at me. "My men are the best warriors in the world. They can handle these creatures easily. You are a woman and you don't know the ways of men. You were lucky when you fought the two dragons. You better remember your place."

"You know best," was all I said in reply.

Chapter Thirteen

After we had been at the island for eight days and had replenished our supplies of food and water, we set sail for Cleopatra. As we sailed northeast, we came upon a huge shark, easily twenty feet long. We thought we had seen it before, just before we spotted the island for the first time. When a sailor on the Chin junk tried to harpoon it, it swam away with the harpoon in its back. We were surprised by the strength and speed of the shark. It swam just off their stern for more than an hour before heading back to its feeding grounds. Many of the sailors on board the *May's Rose* felt it was a bad omen for the junk.

Three days later, we ran into a storm that lasted eight days. It was not as strong as the one we'd run into the last time we were sailing in these waters. It did cause some worries, though. We had prepared for high seas and did not lose anyone, but we had some close calls. Four of our sailors lost their footing, but the captain had ordered lifelines to be strung just before the storm hit, and this saved them from a watery grave. I never found out how it affected the Chin junk. I think they lost one or two of their crew.

The next three days were pleasant, with gentle rolling waves and good winds at our back. When we spotted seabirds late on the third day, we knew the land was near.

Our ship's lookout was the first to spot Cleopatra's lighthouse the next morning.The whole crew was overjoyed.We anchored in the harbor, near one of themerchant landings.The town turned out to see who had arrived from the Far East.

The weather was not as hotasit had been before.The people were friendly, but as before, I sensed a certain aloofness in them, as if they were overly proud oftheir culture and past glories.Ambassador Lee's ship arrived about fifteen minutes after we anchored.He had his sampan in the water within minutes of dropping anchor.He obviously was in a big hurry to meet with. We learned later that he met with General Longius, who was now Procurator of Cleopatra.

Since we had been there before, we knew that during the middle of the day, everyone liked to stay inside and out of the sun.We took that time to open our cargo holds and get some of the cargo ready to be sent to market. We also sent ashore the two survivors from the island, Quintus Atius Remus and Titus Claudius Romulus.We saw them four days later boarding a Tullian merchant ship.

On the first afternoon, I went to the public baths during the women's time.I did the normal things like the rest of the women who went to the baths. After washing, I swam in a pool of cold water before going to the hot pool to soak.Most of the local women who were in the hot pool were aloof, but some seemed friendly and smiled. I ignored the women who were talking in whispers and pointing at me. After several minutes, an older upper-classwoman came over to me. I cast a language spell so we could talk.She was surprised I knew magic.She introduced herself as General Longius's wife, Catilla.She had several questions about me and my adventures.

"Howcan youlive with so many men and never have sex or marry any of them?" she asked. "And is it true that you personally killed two huge dragons singlehanded? Are you truly a magical creature called an elf?"

I answered her questions as best I could, starting with the explanation that I had begun sailing with my uncle, captain of *May's Rose*, and that the crew had always treated me more like a kid sister than a woman.As for the two dragons, I killed the young red dragon myself, but I had help from some great warriors with the dragon lich.And I was only half elf.And although a good number of elves could wield magic, many could not.

As I spoke, more of the other women came nearer to hear my tales of adventure.

"I have heard of this dragon lich," Catilla said. "Ambassador Chan Lee told my husbandabout it. He said youled a company of Chin soldiers and a handful of samurais to victory over thehuge ancient undead dragon. The dragon was forty-five feet long and breathed an ice storm that could freeze a man in seconds.His claws were the size of a sword and could slice iron armor to shreds with one swipe."

I thought I should correct her but decided to tell her that it was true.I showed her my scar from where Berubazius's claw had pierced my armor.I also said we lost half of the soldiers in the battle. One woman asked about my battle with the red dragon, and I told that story as well. In fact, I talked most of the time the women had control of the bathhouse.Catilla asked me to return the next day to tell more tales.

The next day, I returned to the baths.After I had washed, Catilla sought me out. She asked again what it was like working and living with so many men.

"Most of the sailors," I said, "have wives or sweethearts, and I know those women. So the men know I could easily tell on them if they tried anything."

"Did those without wives, did they try to bed you?" Catilla asked.

"Yes, five of them," I said. "But our Second Mate Irvin Ashman, out of true loyalty to my uncle, put end to that. I have to say, their pickup lines were either pretty old or pretty bad."

Catilla laughed.

Another woman joined us and asked, "Did they show their tools? How big were they?"

I frowned. "I never thought much about their tools.They have about the same tools that most sailors have, like amarline spike, a knife or two, a hand ax.Some have weapons, like spears or swords."

"No," the woman said. "Don't you know what makes a man different from a woman?"

"Yes," I said, refusing to be drawn into this conversation. "And I knowmost of my crewmates are married and off limits."

Catilla glared at the other woman and turned back to me. "But now you have lost your uncle. Did he leave you well provided?"

"He left me all he owns—his ship, house, his share of the profits from this voyage."

"Is that all he left you?" Catilla asked.

"I do have the trading rights to the Ryujin port of Izeki, the Chin port of Po Hsien, and the Wei port of Zhang.My name is listed on all three company's trade charters."

"Who else is listed on the trade charters?" Catilla asked.

"On the charters for Chin and Wei, Captain Greenleaf and Captain Mattock," I said. "But on Ryujin, it's me and First Mate Hardwood."

Catilla switched topics. "I heard your company saved Mr. Quintus Atius Remus and Senator Titus Claudius Romulus from a group of small lizard men.Is this true?"

"Yes, we found them in a ghost town on an island we discovered on the way to Wei," I said.

"Is your company allied with Senator Titus Claudius Romulus and Mr. Quintus Atius Remus?" Catilla asked.

Her many questions were making me nervous. "No, but I believe they are allied with Captain Loc and his company."

"Mr. Lee said that your company has a map that shows the trade route to the Far East. If this is true, how much would you want for a copy of the map?" Catilla asked.

"I can't say," I said. "Our company leader is the only one that can sell a copy of the map."

"But Mr. Lee said you are the Pilot of the *May's Rose*.As the ship's Navigator, don'tyou have a copy of the map?" Catilla said to me.

I looked directly at her. "I have access to the copied maps, but the Captain keeps them all under lock and key.Why do you want a copy of the map to the Far East?"

"As you know, anyone with that map could make a fortune," Catilla said. "I plan to make a fortune for myself and become independent."

For the next fivedays that we were in port, I returned to the baths and found more women wanting to hear my tales.One woman asked if Iwanted to fight in the local arena with the gladiators.I told her that I was happy being the pilot and navigator of the *May's Rose*.

By the time we left Cleopatra, we had tradeda hundred and fifty bolts of silk and one hundred and twenty pieces of white and green jade for provisions. Wehad also acquired one hundred and sixty ivory tusks, a chest of different types of gems, thirty chests of different spices, and fifty pounds of gold. We set sail forTullian in a convoy withAmbassador Lee's junk, twenty-four other merchant ships, and two Tullianwar galleys.

The next three days were sunny with gently rolling seas. The wind from the north was cool.We knew there were pirates out there, but we caught no sight of them.On the fourth day, our lookouts spotted them, but their ships quickly moved out of sight.Captain Mattockthought they would strike at dust or at night.He allowed each of the crew to sleep during the day to prepare for the night's action.

He was right!They came from the west, which put the setting sun in our eyes.We raised our battle banner, and I cast a ball of magical energy at their largest ship.When it struck, the whole world lit up.Some of their ships fired catapults, but others ran away.It was a sight to see.Their plan just fell apart within minutes. All their shots fell short of us.One did hit Mr. Lee's ship but did little damage.Within minutes, we saw only their sternsas they raised every inch of sail their masts could hold.Captain Mattock laughed as the crew cheered, shouting insults at the pirates.One of the war galleys started to chase them, but the pirates had too much of a head start, and it returned.

Captain Mattockasked Arion, our translator, to inform the war galley's commander that we had hit the pirates with magic, as we had done the last time, they attacked us.We had sunk all but three of their shipsthattime, and he guessed they had learned their lessons.

The war galley's commander laughed and gave orders to return to their assigned spot in the convoy.We kept extra lookouts on watch through the night, but for the rest of the voyage, we had no more sight of pirates.

Chapter Fourteen

T he last day of the voyage to Tullian dawned cold and rainy. By midday, we saw the entrance of the city's harbor. Shore officials led us to an anchorage away from the docks. It did not matter to us, but we wanted to know what was going on. We learned that there were elections that week. This could be dangerous for us since we were considered barbarians, which could hurt either side in the political campaign. This put a damper on my plans to visit the baths while we were in port.

As for Mr. Lee, his ship did tie up to a pier, and I saw him disembark and go into the city. We saw him only a few times after that.

The next day, we were allowed to tie up to one of the merchant's piers so we could trade. Only Arion and Hektor could leave the pier so they could visit their families. Both asked to stay with the company but asked for their pay. Captain Greenleaf paid them what they'd earned to date so they could give the money to their families. They returned two days later.

On the fifth day after we hit port and with all our trading done, we set the night anchor watch, and most of the crew went below to bed. In two days, we would raise anchor and sail home. I stayed on deck to watch the beautiful sunset and the stars rising. As I was looking at the stars, I dreamed of home. I remembered my birthday parties, when mother baked me a cake and my uncle came with gifts from foreign ports. I also thought of our shipmates who would neverreturn home from this voyage. Had the journey been worth it?I could see all their faces, including my uncle's.He had believed this voyage was worth it, and that it was necessary.

With tears in my eyes,I turned to go below.I was surprised to see Roland standing nearby.

"Bess," he said,"do you have something in your eyes?"

"No,Roland.I was just remembering our lost shipmates who will never return home.I will see you in the morning."

With that, I went to my cabin and bed.

The sound of someone trying to open my cabin door woke me from a light sleep.I always locked the door and placed a small wooden bar across it to hold it shut.My uncle had ordered me to do thatevery time I went to sleep.

An unknown voice speaking in an old common dialect called to me. "Open your door. The ship owner and shipmaster needyour service, Miss Elizabeth Rose Silverleaf.They want to see you now.We will escort you to them."

"I see," I answered."I will need a few minutes to get dressed."

I prepared for a fight.I put on my damagedelfin chainmail and grabbed my long sword and main gauche.I figured the battle would be a close-quarters fight.

After a few minutes, whoever was out there apparently realized I wasn't going to open the door.They struck at the door, probably trying to break it down with their shoulders.I pointed toward the door and chanted an ancient lullaby. Plucking some loose-down feathers from my pillow, I blew them toward the door, an old sleep charm I'd learned from my father's people. I heard a couple of thuds beyond my door indicating at least two of the intruders had fallen asleep. Still, the banging on the door continued, until they managed to open it up a crack.

"Intruders!" I shouted."We are under attack!"

One man tried to break through the crack in my door. "You will come with me now!"

I stabbed him with my sword through the crack in the door.He fell back as I pulled out my sword.His blood sprayed everywhere as he said something I did not understand.

I unlocked my door and pulled it open, ready to fight the other men,as Captain Mattock stepped out of his cabin,swinging his sword at one of the intruders.

"What are you doing on my ship?" Captain Mattock yelled.

"We came to take this woman and all maps you have," the man said as he drew his sword.

The Captain laughed. "So, you thief, prepare for the fight of your life."

The man parried Captain Mattock's first strike, but before he could do more, another man cried out a warning. "The crew is stirring, and we must go."

The man must have decided he'd met his match, for he followed the other man toward the stairs to the main deck. As he reached the top, he must have run into something because he fell onto the deck. Following Captain Mattock up the stairs, I saw Mr. Hardwood standing there with a bloodied fist.

The first man was still lying on the deck, with blood coming from his mouth. Captain Mattock pointed his sword's point at the man's throat. "Stave fast and call your men to drop their weapons, or you are dead."

By now the rest of the crew had come running, some with weapons in hand. A few grabbed the intruders, tying them up. As they started for the brig, we all saw the bodies of our anchor watch. Our friends and shipmates lay on the deck, killed by the intruders. Roland's throat had been cut. Egan had been strangled; a rope tied around his neck. William had had his skull crushed. We lined all five intruders on the starboard railing as the crew shouted for their deaths. Captain Mattock had a hard time controlling them. He did not want us to be known as barbarians.

He was interrupted by a call from the lookout. The *Spring Flower* was under attack.

"To arms!" Captain Mattock called. "Prepare for battle. All hands to your post. They shall not take the *Spring Flower*!"

Before we could go to the *Spring Flower*'s aid, her crew had repelled the invaders. One of the intruder's boats tried to row away, but I cast a sleep spell that knocked all the men unconscious. The *Spring Flower* launched its longboat to recover the sleeping men.

Captain Mattock ordered four of the crew to prepare our fallen shipmates for burial. "Remember," he added, "we are not barbarians. We follow the law." He turned to me. "Are you all right? We need to fix your door in the morning." Before I could answer, he shouted out another order. "Mr. Hardwood! You have someone repair Miss Elizabeth's door first thing in the morning. She will sleep in my cabin the rest of tonight."

"Aye, sir," Mr. Hardwood answered. "I will have my best man on it in the morning."

Captain Mattock replied, "Good. When Captain Greenleaf arrives, we will know what we can do with these assassins.The company will have *JUSTICE*for our dead shipmates." He turned to me again. "Miss ElizabethRose Silverleaf! Join me on the quarterdeck."

"Aye, aye, sir,"I answered as I walked behind him to the quarterdeck.

Captain Mattock turned soquickly;I almost ran into him.He gave another order. "Mr. Hardwoodhave the next watch take over now. I will not have this happen again to my ship and men."

"Aye, Captain Mattock."Mr. Hardwood turned to Aldrich. "Mr. Aldrich, you will assume Mr. Roland's duties as second mate now. You take the anchor watch.Keep your eyes open."

Mr. Hardwood turned toward the crew. "Go below!" he ordered."We need to prepare to this ship for sea."

Although a few men disappeared below, most did not. They stayed on deck, ready for anything.

Captain Mattock, Mr. Hardwood, and I stood on the quarterdeck looking at the crew, the stars, and the harbor.Our presence kept the crew under control. WhenCaptain Greenleaf arrived, the whole crew assembled without being called to quarters.Through Arion, Captain Greenleaf asked our captured men who had sent them and what theywere to achieve.After the man spoke, AriontoldCaptain Greenleafthat the men were the property of the family of Gaius, and he could not kill them without his permission.

"And what about the ones who attackedthe *Spring Flower*?" Captain Greenleaf asked.

Arion answer, "They are also property of Gaius and we cannot kill them without his permission, but the state could."

Captain Greenleaf stated angrily, "Good. Send for the authorities and Mr. Gaius. I will have justice for my murderedcompany members and crew."

Arion and two members of the crew wentashore to find the authorities and Mr. Gaius.After half an hour,they returned with twentysoldiers, one judge, and Mr. Gaius, along withfive members of his household.

Through Arion, Captain Greenleaftold them what had happened. "We brought you here for justice for the murdered members of our company," he finished."We will not accept a barbarian act of murder against our company."

The judge, whose name was Aulus, looked shocked and was speechless. But Mr. Gaius had something to say.

"My slaves did what?" he began in a loud voice. "They acted on their own, for their own goal. This wasnotany goal of my family. My family condemns their action and had nothing to do with these crimes."

Judge Aulusfound his voice, and it was much calmer than Gaius's. "The State is sorry for your loss of sevenof your men and the attempted kidnapping of one of your sailors."

Captain Greenleafgestured to the captured men. "These servants say we cannot punish them because they belong to Gaius. What punishment are you going to do to them?"

"I will allow the state to punish these slaves," Gaius said. "Were they able to steal any of your weapons?I know I must pay for damage my slaves have done."

"No," Mr. Hardwood said. "All our weapons are accounted for, but here are their weapons."Hepointed to a pile of weapons. "Did you know they called Miss Silverleafby her full name?"

"By her name?" Aulus said. "Centuriontake these slaves into custody.Let them bequestioned according to the law.I need to know who supported them, where they got these weapons, and how did knew Miss Silverleaf's name.And why did they want Miss Silverleaf."

The Centurion gathered up the weapons and took Gaius'sslaves away.All the slaves begged for mercy from Gaius and Aulus.Neitherwas moved to help them or provide any mercy.

Judge Aulus turned to us. "After questioning, if they don't provide any answers, I will pronounce they received a fair trial, which should last about an hour.If found guilty, thenext daythey will be taken to Execution Hill. There theywill be crucified for their crime."

"Justice will be done,"Captain Mattock said. He looked at the crew. "Go below!There is nothing else to be done here now."

The next day, we all rose early to meet the morning. True to his word, Judge Aulus had all ten murderers led to a hill onthe North side of the town and crucified.We spent the rest of the day preparing to sail on the next morning's first tide.Captain Greenleaf planned to bury our fallen shipmates at sea.Mr. Lee sent his regrets of our losses. He would not be traveling on with us. He was staying in Tullian to setup anEmbassy for the Chin Empire.

I wondered who had sent theintruders.Gaius? Quintus Atius Remus? Titus Claudius Romulus? Rowen Loc? Pirates? Or someone else I did not know?

At the end of the day, a young girl, about seven years old and carrying a large sack, walked up the gangway and asked for Hektor. When he saw her, Hektor ran up to her and gave her a hug. Then he took her to Captain Mattock.

"Captain," he said, "with your permission, I would like to take my daughter to Fair Haven on board the *May's Rose*. May I have your permission to bring her with us? I will share my food with her."

"You know there are dangers out there on the high sea," Captain Mattock said.

"She does not have a place to live. I work without pay so she can come with us."

The girl looked at her father with puzzlement. She no doubt didn't understand what he was saying. She said nothing herself.

The Captain scowled at Hektor. "You will work for half pay, and she will stay with Miss Elizabeth. She will obey and help Miss Elizabeth with her job. Is this clear?"

"Aye, Captain. She will be a good girl and stay with Miss Elizabeth." Hektor smiled at his daughter.

For the second time, I had someone with me in my cabin. The girl said nothing that night. She acted like I was going to beat her any second.

As the sun rose over the sea the next morning, we unmoored from the pier and set sail for home. The sky was clear with only a few clouds. Everyone was happy with the idea of soon being home with loved ones. They were all looking forward to the end of this dangerous journey of adventure. The crew sang the sea shanties with a joy I had not heard since we'd started this voyage. With the wind out of the west, we were able to make good speed, about five to seven knots.

The fine weather lasted for five days, but by the sixth day, we saw a change. A storm was coming. We prepared for the worst and hoped for the best. The storm lasted eight days, but we did not lose a single man. We gave thanks to our gods.

As the thirteenth day ended, we could see stars to guide us. We sailed through the night with the gentle roll of the ship. Fair winds and calm sea to our backs lifted our hearts. By morning, we were joined by a school of dolphins playing at the bows of both ships. To most of the crew, this was a good omen, and so it was.

For the next nine days, the weather was good.We spotted several pods of whales, but we kept an eye out for large squids, remembering the one that had attacked the *Raven*.Though we never saw any, we knew they were around.

On the twenty-second day, we saw the remains of *Zaria*.I figured we were seven days from home.That night, as I took watch, I found most of the crew was having trouble sleeping.Instead of being in their bunks, they were on deck staring out to sea. This worriedme, since I knew a tired man was more likely to make mistakes or have an accident.

When CaptainMattockcame on deck, I asked him if we should be concernedthat the crew was having trouble sleeping.

"Nothing to worry about," he said."It's a common illness on ships when they've made a long journey from home.I expected it to happen earlier than this."

Overhearing our conversation, Gibbon joined us. "It may infect the whole crew before long, even you.The only cure is docking in your home port."

The next two days were uneventful, but on the twenty-fifth day since we'd left Tullian, we saw sails off in the distance.As we sailed closer, we could see it was our fishing fleet.They had spotted ustoo and cheered when they drew close enough to recognize us.We were their friends, who had sailed for an adventure and wealth.They called out the names of their friends and kinsman who had sailed with our company.Too many of the requests were answered with, "He is dead."But we were able to givesome happier answers thatthe man they asked after was alive, well, and had returned with treasures from the Far East.

We asked about the *Raven* and learned shenever made it back.That was a blow to us, but the sea was a dangerous place.More of our fishing fleet came near to cheer us home.Some had filled their holds, and they joined us on the last leg of our journey.

Our last night at sea was different from what I'd expected.The crew cleaned the ship and sang songs from home with joy.I saw men break out their best clothes, and some even washed for the first time in a long time.We ate a hearty meal, and no one could sleep—with one exception. The little girl in my cabin.

Chapter Fifteen

Near noon the next day, we could see the lighthouse at the entrance of our home port. A bell rang out, and then another, and then another. Soon we could hear every bell in town. The docks filled with the whole town. It was a wonderful sight. Cheers came from everyone!

Mr. Hardwood came up to me as we sailed into the port. "What are your plans for the night? Are you going to see some of your father's kinfolk if they're in town?"

"No," I answered. "My uncle was my last kinsman in Fair Haven."

"Then you will come home with me for a real home-cooked meal. My mother would love it. I will not take no for an answer."

Captain Mattockhad walked up behind us, and he spoke. "Mr. Hardwood, you are right. Miss Silverleaf needs a good home-cooked meal. She owns a good ship and a map to the treasures of the Far East. Plus, she's not a bad looker to boot." He grinned at us, and then he shouted, "You two get back to work! This is not a pleasure ship. Get working. We are sailing to our home port and need to look professional."

As soon as we docked and lowered the gangway, townsfolk swarmed onto the ship. Everyone was being hugged and kissed. It took some time to tie off the ship and break the crew down to the anchor watch.

Before any of the crew left the ship, the town's guards came on board. "Where is Mr. Ervin Claymore?" the sergeant in charge asked. "We have orders to take him into custody."

Captain Mattock walked up to the sergeant. "Mr.Claymore died in a battle at a port in Ryujin."

"We know he was planning to make a map of this journey," the Sergeant said. "Where is his master map?"

"Captain Greenleaf of the *Spring Flower* may have it," Captain Mattock saidhaltingly.

The Sergeant said, "Thank you.We also knowhe had an apprentice.What happened to him?"

I stepped up to speak, but Mr. Hardwood stopped me.

"Aye, he had one," Captain Mattock said. "Why do you want the apprentice?"

The Sergeant said, "I have orders to take him into custody for questions and his protection, by the order of the Captain of the Guard."

Captain Mattock looked at me. "Miss Silverleaf studied under Mr. Claymore."

The Sergeant laughed. "You're pulling my leg.She is a woman and she could not learn to be a pilot or cartographer.Now be serious. Did he have anyone he was training as cartographer?"

Captain Mattock started to speak, but I cut him off. "Captain Mattock, Mr. Hardwood would like to help me to move my gear to my uncle's home. Would you mind if I do it now?"

"I see no reason to object," he answered. "If the Sergeant doesn't have any objection?"

"I don't have problem with this woman going ashore," the Sergeant said in an angry tone.

The captain nodded to me. "Go ahead and move your gear before something prevents you.Mr. Hardwood, help MissSilverleaf."

"Aye, sir," we both said and went below to pick up my gear.We saw Hektor and his daughter in my cabin.

"Thank you for your help," Hektor said to me.

"What did I do for you?" I asked.

"I used your name to buy my daughter from her master," Hektor said.

"What?" I exclaimed. "You bought your daughter from slavery?Well, at least you used my name for a great cause.But don't do it again! Unless you let me know beforehand."

"Aye, Miss Bess!"both said to me.

When we returned to the main deck, Captain Mattock said to the Sergeant, "If you believe she was not trainable for the job of a cartographer, then I have no one else to point to you. Have a good day."

The Sergeant looked surprised but did not say anything.

Gibbon and I walked down the gangplank, reaching the dock just as the Captain of the Guard arrived. He stood at the foot of the gangplank and shouted up at his sergeant.

"Sergeant! I have Mr. Claymore's maps.Have you found Mr. Claymore's apprentice? His name is Mr. E. R. Silverleaf."

"No," the Sergeant called back down. "There is no one by that name.The only SilverleafisElizabeth Rose Silverleaf, who just passed you on the pier."

The Captain of the Guards turned quickly toward Gibbon and me. "You two guards, stop her."He pointed at me. "Miss Silverleaf, you stop there.You need to come with me."

I stopped and turned to face him. "Your Sergeant said I was not the one you were looking for," I said calmly."I also cleared that with my ship'sCaptain before departing the ship.Now why do you want a helpless woman?"

"You are not a helpless woman," he said."By all accounts, you are some sort of wizard warrior who can handle herself in battle, and you killed two dragons. Also, you acted as this company's mapmaker after Mr. Claymore's death and may have the most updated world map in your custody.With CaptainLoc in town, we need to lock you up for your and the town's protection.So, will you be following me to the castle, or will I lock you up in jail?Your choice."

Captain Loc stepped onto the pier from *Spring Flower*. "She has nothing to worry about.I would need a ship to sail away with her."

The Captain of the Guards pointed atCaptain Loc and angrily said, "You stay out of this.I will have to protect her from you."

"Why?" Captain Loc asked. "She is single, and my third son is also single.I think it is a good match."

Mr. Hardwood looked at Captain Loc and said, "No. She is mine.Keep your hands off."

"I have my orders," the Captain of the Guard said in a commanding voice."You all stay out of this.She will come with me.The king will make the final decision as towho will take control of her and the map."

Within seconds,I was surrounded by six city guards. "Sergeant," the Captain of the Guards ordered,"you and your men are to guard the *May's Rose* and this pier untilI send your replacement."

The Captainled me away to the town's castle and palace of the king.

As we approached the castle, I could see a well-dressed man on the battlements.

"Whereis Mr. Ervin Claymore?" he shouted down to theCaptain."And who is this woman?"

"Mr. Claymore is dead," the Captain answered,"but I have his master map.She was his apprentice."

"His apprentice?Captain,take her to the north tower, and place her under guard."

The Captain said he would and took me to a room near the topof the north tower. He took all my weapons and my spell books, but he left my sea chest.

"May I have paper and ink to write my adventures?" I asked."I need to keep my hands and mind busy."

"I see no reason why not," he said."It will cost you some coins for the papers and ink.But I need to see your map."

"Then search me and my sea chest, if you like.I have nothing to hide."

He searched me and my sea chest, but he did not find my map."Where is the map?"he asked.

"I do not have a paper copy of Mr. Claymore's map.I gave it to Captain Greenleaf."

"CaptainGreenleaf gave me Mr. Claymore's map.Now where is your map?"

"You searched me, and I don't have what you're looking for.Please let me go," I said.

"Not until the king says you can go."As he left the room, he turned back and asked, "Does Captain Loc have your map? Or does Captain Mattock have it?"

"No.I never letCaptain Locsee any of our company's maps.I do not have a paper copy of Mr. Claymore's mapsbecause I never made a paper copy of the map for myself.So Captain Mattock has never seen any paper copy of the map of the Far East."

"I will check your cabin and Captain Loc.He will never get that map." The Captain closed and locked the door tomy room.

I was given paper and ink the next day, and I started to write this tale of my adventures of the quest of *May's Rose*.It kept me busy, and I was able honor the ones who had died on the journey.

After two weeks in the North Tower, King Geoffrey came to see me. He was the well-dressed man I'd seen on the battlements when I was led to the castle.

"Do you know me?" he asked as he entered my room. "I'm Geoffrey, the King of West Thorne. Your cabin on the *May's Rose* has been searched. The guards could not find any sight of the map you made from Mr. Claymore. I've been informed your person and belongings have been searched as well."

"Do you believe I made a copy of Mr. Claymore's map?" I asked.

"Yes, I believe you did. I also have no reason to hold you. Captain Loc and his company left on one of his country's ships yesterday. If you have the map of the trade route and you keep it secret from everyone, then my kingdom is safe."

He was right that I did have a copy of Mr. Claymore's map. The truth was I was wearing it as a petticoat beneath my dress. Mr. Claymore had warned me to keep my map well hidden and never tell anyone that I had it. He had been right. If he'd known for sure I had the map, the king would have kept me locked up or under guard for the rest of my life. Instead, he let me go, and I returned to my uncle's home.

I found the king had sold Mr. Claymore's map to one of the local cartographers. The cartographer had paid handsomely for it, from the stories I heard.

My share of the journey's profits was a great fortune. I also found my uncle had had a new type of ship designed and built when he was away, one of the shipwrights in town had completed her. She was a galley, bigger than the *May's Rose*, and could hold more cargo and passengers. I must name her before her chiseling and launch in two weeks.

As for Captain Greenleaf and Captain Mattock, they were planning to go back to the East by the route we discovered. They want me to go along as one of the pilots. I told them I would think about it.

As for Captain Rowen Loc, he returned to Gyrlac. He wrote to me to tell me he will never set sail again as a Sea Captain, but he would like me to take his third son on my next adventure. I am considering it since I think it could lead to peace and a joint adventure between our two kingdoms. Of course, I know he still plans to marry me to his third son so he can get his hands on my fortune and my maps of the trade route to the Far East.

I did finally make it to Mr. Gibbon Hardwood's home for a home-cooked meal. His mother had already found him a wife. She was a childhood friend. Gibbon had chased her for years, until she caught him. I gave them a wedding gift—a set of dishes with flowers that I found in Po Hsien—and I wish them a happy and good life together.

I'm still very young and have time for more adventures before I get tied down.

Our warehouses are full of treasures of the East, weopened a new trade route, and every one of our company is now rich and famous.

AsIstand at the head of the breakwater looking out to the sea, I am thinking of my next adventure.I feel the pull of the sea in my heart, like Mr. Hill warned me at the beginning of the journey. He and my uncle were right.Once you get the salt of the sea in your blood, you are drawn to go to sea again.

Spell Caster – A wizard, one who can cast magic

Careening—when a ship is brought out of the water to clean the keel (the bottom of a ship, below the water level) of sea growth

Procurator—Military governor of a territory

Prize Crew—Sailors who take of a captured enemy ship to a friendly port for money from the sailing of the ship

Warcaster—A spell caster and warrior; can cast spells,is trained in using weapons and ware armor

Starboard—the right side of a ship

Port—theleft side of a ship

Leeward – An old term for left side of the ship, and opposite of windward

Windward—the side or direction from which the wind is blowing (e.g., the windward side of the island) most time.